DANGER IN THE DESERT

Hired to guard gold being shipped by stagecoach, Matt Nylund's job is complicated by concern for the safety of passengers who include an arrogant lawyer and an elderly preacher, who are travelling with their women. When the stage is held up, the gold stolen and the coach set on fire, Nylund and his charges are stranded in the burning desert. In his determination to find water, bring the passengers to safety and recover the gold, Nylund has to contend with dangerous interference from the bombastic lawyer as well as ferocious natural dangers and the merciless guns of bandits.

DANGER IN THE DESERT

DANGER IN THE DESERT

by

Terry Murphy

Dales Large Print Books
Long Preston, North Yorkshire,
BD23 4ND, England.

British Library Cataloguing in Publication Data.

Murphy, Terry
Danger in the desert.

A catalogue record of this book is
available from the British Library

ISBN 978-1-84262-511-8 pbk

First published in Great Britain in 1992 by Robert Hale Ltd.

Published in Large Print 2007 by arrangement with
Robert Hale Limited

Dales Large Print is an imprint of Library Magna Books Ltd.

Printed and bound in Great Britain by
T.J. (International) Ltd., Cornwall, PL28 8RW

ONE

Taking the occasional sip from the glass of rye he held in a hand resting on the table in front of him, Matt Nylund sat alone in the crowded, noisy saloon. His corner seat allowed him the opportunity to survey both those who were already in the saloon and those who entered through the bat-wing doors.

Never before had he seen a larger collection of desperadoes and criminals gathered together in one place. Broken noses and disarranged features were commonplace among the fifty or so men that thronged in the small room with its sawdust-covered floor. A reeking mixture of sweat, whisky and tobacco smoke assaulted his nostrils, churning his stomach.

'All aboard. All aboard.'

The harsh, rattling voice carried from the street outside to reach Nylund's ears. Downing the final drop of rye as he stood, and placing the empty glass on the table, he made the short trip across to the door, easing his way through the horde of unclean and jostling bodies that lined the bar four deep.

'Watch your step!' a diminutive cow-puncher mouthed as he, in an uncontrolled, drunken reel, thudded backwards into Nylund. He swallowed his words in a nervous gulp as the big man glared down at him angrily. Nylund's glowering features demanded an apology, and his long, thick fingers curled into huge lethal fists while he waited.

'Sorry,' the smaller man murmured, the whisky-induced bravado having swiftly deserted him.

The almost imperceptible nod of the head from Nylund meant the apology was accepted and the incident forgotten. It was over as quickly as it had started.

Swinging his bag and bedroll up to the man who was securing the luggage on top of the stagecoach Nylund climbed aboard, and, as the last passenger, pulled the door shut behind him.

'Mornin'.' Nylund touched his hat in greeting to his fellow passengers.

They each, in their own way, acknowledged him with a word or a nod of the head.

Stretching out his long legs and settling into his seat, Nylund pulled down the rim of his hat so that it almost covered his eyes but still allowed him to study the five people who would be making the journey with him.

Sitting directly opposite Nylund was a well-dressed young man, a watch and chain hanging from the pocket of his waistcoat. A pretty blue-eyed blonde sat alongside him. Newly-weds, Nylund would wager; travelling out west with high hopes and impossible dreams. They would come scurrying back east in under a year, he was sure, as long as they could then afford the fares for the stagecoach ride. Nylund had seen it all before, their expectations would be shattered by harsh realities; he pitied them.

The new bride, though obviously very much in love and resting her dainty hand possessively on the arm of her husband, cast a flirtatious look in Nylund's direction, the attraction he held for her, being a manly and rugged contrast to her wiry-framed spouse, clearly evident. At one time Nylund would have returned her look, but that was a lifetime ago, when he'd been a different man.

At Nylund's side an elderly preacher dozed, his grey-stubbled chin against his chest, while clutched in his bony fingers, and wrapped discreetly in brown paper, was a quarter-full bottle of whisky, no doubt, thought Nylund cynically, for medicinal purposes.

Beside the preacher sat his stern-faced, staid wife, a copy of the Good Book in her hands, the yellowing, dog-eared pages open at the gospels.

'Why are you going out west, my son?' The

preacher suddenly awoke, and launched himself into a conversation that Nylund assumed must have been running before he boarded. The old man spoke to a freckly-faced youngster who sat across from him. The boy couldn't have been more than thirteen years old.

'Please, sir, I'm going to live with my pa.' The boy, in obvious fear of the man of the cloth, whispered his answer in a quaking voice.

For a second it seemed the preacher was going to probe further; but, dismissing the idea, he turned his questioning on the young couple.

'And you, my children, why are you making such a trip?'

The old preacher's eyes travelled down the young woman, coming to rest on her exposed ankle, which she, cheeks reddening with embarrassment, quickly covered with her long skirt.

'I'm going out west to work,' the man told him proudly and eagerly. 'I hope to make a better life for my wife and myself. We've only been married for a month.'

'Then may the Lord in His wisdom grant you a long and happy life.' With a hint of rambling caused by liquor, the preacher gave them his blessing. 'And what would your work be?'

'I'm an attorney,' the man answered, his peacock feathers making another appearance.

'And you?' The preacher's bloodshot eyes travelled in Nylund's direction. 'We know why everyone else is making the trip; for myself I'm taking up a new post at a recently built chapel. So, what is your business?'

'My own, which I don't plan on discussing,' Nylund told him politely, yet still firmly. The old man got the message straight away. Turning to his wife he took the book from her, delving into its pages to escape any possible further confrontation with the stranger sitting beside him.

Across the coach the pretty blonde raised the corners of her mouth in a smile directed at Nylund, which, this time, he returned, much to the annoyance of her husband.

Nylund turned his face away from the other passengers; he needed neither their company nor their approval. Aware that both angry and interested eyes were watching him, Nylund tried to pay no attention as the Wells Fargo gold box was loaded onto the coach.

TWO

Nylund slept. The gentle rocking of the stagecoach had induced a relaxation in him, yet he was still alert. A tingle of energy ran through his body at all times, allowing him to be fully conscious and aware of his surroundings in a split second.

Waking, Nylund kept his eyelids shut, concentrating on the sounds and voices going on around him. From across the stagecoach he could hear the whispering tones of the young married couple, their words indistinguishable.

A rhythmic breathing and occasional snort was a clear indication that the preacher was asleep too. The religious man's wife was talking to, or rather at, the youngster, who had only the briefest of breaks in her sentences in which to answer in monosyllables.

Nylund thought that soon the boy would be feigning sleep, just to escape the continuous drone of the woman's voice.

Opening his eyes, Nylund pulled his timepiece from his pocket, surprised to learn he had been asleep for only an hour. To him it seemed longer, but he had the ability to recover both his mental and physical strength after only a brief rest.

The bright sun that shone into the stagecoach caused the brooch on the dress of the attorney's beautiful young wife to sparkle. The facets of the jewels cast their reflective beams in all directions. The couple, Nylund realized, were not strangers to wealth. That one brooch probably cost more money than had passed, albeit fleetingly, through Nylund's own hands in the previous twelve months.

Aware that Nylund's eyes were on her, the young woman blushed slightly, her cheeks turning pink. Noticing his wife's reaction to the rugged stranger, the attorney shot Nylund an angry glare. A smile played on

Nylund's lips; he was confidently aware that the man wasn't capable of throwing anything more powerful than a look in his direction. It was a cruel twist of nature that some men were born physically strong and others born weak. The attorney was definitely the latter and Nylund the former. Both men were aware where they stood in nature's pecking order.

Having both amused and entertained himself with the brief incident, Nylund closed his eyes again, slipping easily into a light sleep.

The jolt of the stagecoach slowing awoke him. Immediately he identified the sound of a horse's hooves pounding alongside the coach. Instinctively Nylund's hand went to his side. Beneath the long coat he wore he could feel the reassuring shape of his Colt .45.

'Oh no.' The pretty blonde threw her hands to her face in horror. 'It's robbers.'

'Robber, ma'am. In the singular.' Nylund touched his hat, with the same casualness as he had on boarding. 'If you would care to look you'll see just the one man.'

The woman began to stand to do as Nylund suggested, but her husband pulled her back by the arm into her seat, speaking sharply. 'Stay where you are, Daphne, you don't know what sort of ruffians they are.'

'How is it you know there's only one?' the preacher asked accusingly, as if he believed Nylund was in possession of previously obtained information.

'There's only one horse. Or do you suggest there are others on foot?'

'There could be others up ahead, lying in wait with some sort of trap.' Unable to beat him physically the attorney was making an attempt at a mental confrontation.

'Then we wouldn't be stopping here.' Nylund verbally shot the lawyer down, not displeased with his own performance.

'We are poor people. I have nothing worth stealing,' the preacher blubbered, showing a selfish side Nylund considered shouldn't be present in the character of a religious man.

The stagecoach came to a halt, and within

seconds of it stopping the door was thrown open and the barrel of a Winchester rifle appeared in the gap.

'Everybody out and make it quick.' A man's voice, distorted by the neckerchief he wore across his lower face, blurred the order.

No one moved. All were frozen in their seats, either through fear or anger; for Nylund it was the latter. All eyes turned to Nylund, as if expecting a lead from him. Nylund inwardly chuckled. If he were to launch into a roof-raising hymn he was sure all voices would follow. Thoughts practical now, Nylund stood, and slowly, making no sudden movements that would alarm the possibly itchy-fingered bandit, he climbed down from the stagecoach, his legs soon adapting to the solid, stationary ground beneath his feet.

The robber was nervous, Nylund could tell; more frightened maybe than any of his victims. He wasn't that old either, perhaps just half a dozen years or so older than the youngest passenger. His body was jittery with nerves. Transferring his weight from one leg to the other his anxious eyes watched the passengers alight. The patterned neckerchief which prevented Nylund from seeing the robber's full face was damp with sweat, clinging to his lips as he spoke.

'Line up, over there.'

He waved the Winchester away from the stagecoach and toward a small cluster of low rocks where the coach driver and his assistant stood, their hands raised above their heads.

'Move!'

Concentrating on each step, careful not to trip or fall, the passengers kept watching the Winchester barrel as they walked, as if they could anticipate the rifle being fired and avoid being shot.

With the stock of the gun tucked tightly under one arm, the robber released his grip with one hand, taking off his stetson and throwing it toward the young boy passenger. The hat landed neatly at the boy's feet, but he stood rigid, not even bending his neck to look down at the hat which lay partly on one of his boots.

'Pick it up!' barked the rifleman, pulling the neckerchief away from his nostrils as it impaired his breathing.

The boy picked it up, still ignorant as to what was expected of him. The robber didn't know that the boy's inertia was caused by bewilderment and not wilful obstinacy. One more minute of this battle of wills caused by confusion, Nylund thought, and the already agitated robber was going to lose control.

Pulling a ring from his finger, Nylund dropped it into the upturned hat. His simple action told the boy all he needed to know. Each passenger followed suit, removing jewellery and other valuables from their persons and tossing them into the stetson.

'And that.'

Stepping forward the thief prodded the attorney in the chest with the barrel of his rifle.

'And the watch.'

He had caught the glistening of the chain as the lawyer's coat had fallen open.

The attorney's hand flew to his pocket, not, as Nylund first thought, to hand the timepiece over, but to grip it protectively.

'No,' he objected vehemently. 'You are not stealing this. It was given to me by my father when I graduated from law school. It is an heirloom that I intend to hand down to my own son.'

'Give.' The bandit uttered the single word, his inflection full of threat.

'Hand it over, man. It's not worth us all getting killed for.' The preacher blurted out the words.

'No thieving scoundrel is going to take it from me.'

'Thomas,' his pretty wife gasped, seeing the foolhardiness of her husband's actions. 'Let him have it.'

What patience the robber had was now stretching very thin. As he took part in the three-way conflict between himself and passenger, and passenger with passenger, he was growing increasingly angry. Nylund could see his finger twitching close to the trigger and realized that the man was closer now than he ever would be to pulling it. With the attorney standing directly in front of the barrel, there was no doubting who the victim would be.

As he was standing next to the lawyer, Nylund had the perfect opportunity to intervene, and this he did; with a sudden but controlled movement which assured the robber he wasn't Nylund's target, he brought his hand up – and snatched at the chain of the watch, ripping the pocket of the attorney's waistcoat as he tore away the timepiece. In one swift movement he tossed it into the stetson.

'Why you son of a...'

The lawyer's outburst proved that Nylund had successfully achieved his aim, the attorney's anger was now safely directed at the big man standing alongside him, and not at the desperado.

Relaxing his arms at his side again, Nylund was thankful for the robber's naivety in that he didn't have the passengers raise their hands above their heads as he had done the two drivers. In his foolishness he saw no danger to himself from the passengers.

Stepping back two strides the robber distanced himself from his victims. Lowering the rifle barrel slightly he again tucked the stock under one arm, reaching out with the other for the return of his now valuables-laden hat. Whether through stupidity or not, the boy passenger tossed the stetson back to the robber in the very same way he had received it.

In the bandit's position, Nylund would have had the boy pick up the hat from the ground and pass it to him. The robber wasn't so wise. Unaware of how vulnerable his action made him, he stooped to the ground, his fingers grasping the brim of the stetson. He picked up the hat, and began to straighten his body. The man had made a fatal mistake. As he drew himself up he discovered he was facing Nylund's Colt .45. Within a split second Matt Nylund had drawn back his coat and cleared his revolver from the holster.

The man let out a deep gasp, a mixture of shock and fear. Letting the hat slip from his fingers, it fell to the ground, the valuables spilling out. Beside Nylund the attorney's body jerked as if to dive to the ground and retrieve his watch, but an inner self-preservation stopped him from placing himself in the firing line.

Though it seemed to happen slowly, it was really all over within the blink of an eye. Nylund was standing holding a smoking gun and the robber was stretched out on the ground, dark red blood pumping from his chest staining his shirt, the rifle still gripped in his hands.

Checking life was extinguished, Nylund prised the Winchester from the dead man's fingers.

'Was there any need? the preacher asked mournfully, looking deeply at Nylund for his answer. 'Did you have to kill him?'

'A minute ago he was going to kill him.' Nylund thumbed in the attorney's direction. 'And all of us, if needs be. What happened to your eye for an eye, tooth for a tooth, preacher?'

'He was bluffing,' announced the lawyer, not giving any deep thought to the situation he had been facing.

'And you were willing to gamble on that, were you?' Whatever respect Nylund may have had earlier for the lawyer had now completely disappeared.

'There was no real danger,' the attorney scoffed, his attitude more one of bravado than confidence.

Nylund tossed the Winchester to him, the barrel and stock sticky with the dead man's blood.

'That's real enough for me,' Nylund told him pointedly.

The attorney opened his mouth to disagree with Nylund, but then snapped it shut as he realized he had no words with which to argue.

Picking up the stetson from the ground, Nylund held it out for the preacher and his wife to take back their small trinkets, and for the boy to recover the little he had handed over. Putting his own large hand into the hat, Nylund took out the attorney's wife's jewellery, including the many-stoned brooch that had attracted him earlier. Holding out her dainty hand she took her property from Nylund.

'Thank you.' Her voice too low to be heard, she mouthed the words to him. A faint smile played on her lips.

The lawyer turned angrily toward his wife, believing that her simple show of gratitude to the stranger betrayed her loyalty to her husband.

Taking his own ring from the hat, Nylund pushed it back onto his finger, then, with the watch and chain still inside, tossed the stetson across to the attorney. Catching the hat with one hand, the lawyer held the rifle in the other. Looking down at his own hands his face expressed revulsion, as blood from the weapon had stained his fingers. Dropping the rifle to the ground with a crash, the stetson joining it, he ran behind a rock and retched.

THREE

Laying the final stone on the hastily-dug grave of the desperado, Nylund stood, brushing the dirt from the knees of his trousers. The preacher, head bowed, mumbled a brief prayer of thanks for the robber's short life.

'...forever more. Amen.' Slamming the Good Book shut, the preacher gave the grave a quick nod of respect before turning on his heel to head back to the stagecoach, leaving Nylund behind alone at the graveside.

The bandit's face had been familiar to him when Nylund had pulled back the neckerchief. He had felt then as if he had been hit hard in the belly, a blow that caused years to fall away. Had the hold-up youngster been fifteen years older, Nylund would have sworn that he was an old friend of his. Could it just be a similarity in features that had the now dead boy look like a face from the past? Or was it, as seemed even more likely, that the young man he had shot was the son of his old pal? And, even more of a coincidence, that the boy and his father had both lost their lives to bullets from the gun of the same man.

While the preacher, his wife, and the attorney blamed him for unnecessarily killing the man, Nylund saw the two contributing factors to the young man's death clearly. It was obvious, of course, that had the robber not forced the stagecoach to stop, or had not tried to steal from the passengers, then he wouldn't now be lying dead in a shallow grave. Yet he had deliberately held up the stagecoach. What did irritate Nylund, and what was the sole reason, as he saw it, for his needing to shoot the thief, was the attorney's attitude. Refusing to hand over the timepiece had unnecessarily put his own life and the lives of the other passengers at risk.

Anything other than killing the man

straight out would have left him capable of pulling the trigger of the Winchester, something that he surely would have done. How could he explain that to a bunch of do-gooders? Nylund wondered.

Reloading his Colt, Nylund holstered it before walking back to the stagecoach, aware that many pairs of eyes were upon him, watching his every move. Climbing back onto the coach, he found the seating positions had been rearranged. Now he sat next to the boy, on the other side of whom sat the preacher's wife, and opposite them now sat the attorney, his wife and the preacher.

The religious man was slowly turning the pages of his book, perhaps looking for a quotation pertinent to the situation. Pulling at the stitching of his torn waistcoat pocket the attorney's face was glum.

As the coach moved off again it wasn't difficult for Nylund to put the incident out of his mind. Having found it necessary in the past to make a conscious effort to forget unpleasantness, he now found it easy to do so, sometimes too easy.

The cold atmosphere that had been present earlier had chilled even further. Conversation had stopped completely, and even coughs were muffled. No one wanted to break the silence, it was almost oppressive. Nylund was used to being the odd man out. It no longer bothered him, indeed now he thrived on it, believing it was better to have folk hate you than like you; that way you knew where you were. He knew he was in no physical danger from his fellow passengers. This wasn't a saloon where a slip of his guard could end up with his throat being slashed, or some low cattle town where a lonely walk on a dark night could mean trouble. Darn near everyone in the stagecoach wished him harm, yet none had the courage to try to inflict it.

Closing his eyes Nylund tried to sleep, but relaxation wouldn't come to him. The face of the young desperado kept coming back to haunt his thoughts. Trying to push the picture from his mind, he was now unsuccessful.

Over and over the face appeared, at times transposed with that of his old friend. Again he saw the last look Sam had given him, the stark expression of terror in his eyes as he realized Nylund had been quicker on the draw, while his own revolver was still holstered, his hand only just having reached it.

It was a fair fight, there had been no killing in cold blood. They had both gone for their guns at the same time, but Nylund had been the quickest. If Sam had been the speedier of the two, there could be no doubting he would have done the same as Nylund, but, unlike Nylund, he would have fired immediately. To give his friend more of an even chance, Nylund had hesitated. Why, he didn't know; giving a man the opportunity to kill you wasn't a wise idea. As Sam had gone for his revolver, it had been his intention to kill the man facing him. Nylund had squeezed the trigger, sending the man hurtling back across the bar-room table. Glasses crashed to the floor as his sprawling body knocked them from the table.

As the hands of death reached out to grab him the man fired his gun, his finger pulling the trigger in an involuntary seizure, the lead smashing into the wall behind Nylund, missing him by just inches.

Nylund hadn't wanted to harm his friend, but he had been forced into the situation. They had been playing cards, when Sam, a friend for more than five years, with his mind unbalanced by whisky, had wrongly accused Nylund of cheating. There was to be no reasoning with Sam, Nylund discovered. If Nylund hadn't fired it would have been him lying on the saloon floor.

Back at the ranch he had collected his few meagre possessions from the bunkhouse. After a battle of conscience he had returned to town to pay a visit on Sam's half-breed wife.

Opening the door to Nylund, her brown-skinned cheeks tear-stained, and the youngster clinging to her skirts, Mary-Sue had not given him the chance to explain; to apologize. With his face stinging from her vicious slap, Nylund had had the door slammed shut on him.

That was sixteen years ago, but every minute had remained clearly with him. Could it be that now he had brought bereavement to that woman again?

How would the others with whom he was sharing this journey react, Nylund wondered, if they knew that before today he had killed not one man, or two, but half a dozen? The youngster today took the toll to seven. This time it was different, different in that he had done it for free. That would shock them too, to know they were in the company of a paid killer, which was the conclusion they would come to. But they would be wrong. Nylund wasn't paid to kill, he was paid to protect. Whoever threatened to harm his charge, or steal what was in his custody, had to pay the price.

It wasn't for the journey that Nylund was on the stagecoach; he was being paid to make the trip. The stage line, ambushed countless times, was losing the confidence of its high-paying customers. Badly needing a deterrent they had employed Nylund, a man with a reputation that was built mainly on hearsay and unsubstantiated rumour. Nylund doubted if, truthfully, anyone could be capable of all the things that had been said of him. Whatever, he was determined to earn every cent of his substantial fee.

As the haunting image of the young desperado faded and his old memories slowly died down once more, Nylund managed to relax.

There was no need for him to be convivial with the other passengers. It was best for them not to know he was there partly for their safety, and to ensure the safe delivery of the gold that travelled along with them.

With such a valuable cargo on board, there was no doubt in Nylund's mind that they would be ambushed. The only doubt which arose was when.

FOUR

Viewing each passenger one by one, Nylund wondered what he or she would have done during the robbery had he not been present. Though trying not to be egotistical, he felt he had been a calming influence on the group. Certainly, without Nylund the attorney would have been badly injured, if not shot dead by the desperado.

'I hope in your quiet reflection you've had the time to repent your sin.' The preacher spoke, addressing the whole stagecoach rather than Nylund himself.

'Why don't you try to open your mind to what could have happened, rather than what did?' Though not wanting to be drawn into an argument, Nylund was tired of the preacher's attitude towards him.

'You want me to deal with imagination,

rather than reality?' asked the religious man, this time able to look at Nylund.

'I want you to accept the truth,' explained Nylund, trying not to show his annoyance with the man, 'that I shot the robber before he could pull the trigger of his own rifle.'

Not answering, the preacher turned his head way, leaving Nylund uncertain as to whether he had successfully made his point or not.

It had eased Nylund by speaking his mind, but he still didn't know if he had achieved anything, believing the preacher to be too bigoted to accept any opinion other than his own.

Nylund stayed silent, keeping a mental distance from the other passengers. When they halted later, with night rapidly closing in, to change horses for a fresh team, the stagecoach driver took the time to speak to Nylund about the shooting, and he showed the first support Nylund had received for his action.

'We got them darn near every other trip.

Most you can outrun, or the firing of a weapon scares them off.' He shook his white-haired head. 'But I can't remember all the times I've stood looking down the barrel of some robber's rifle, or had the cold mouth of a revolver pressed against my head; then I've truly shaken with fear. I was sure they were going to pull the trigger. Today again it weren't no different. That youngster had killing in his eyes.'

'I know,' Nylund agreed, grateful that the man had spoken to him.

The driver walked away to check on the horses, leaving Nylund standing alone in the moonlit night, dark clouds blowing across the sky, threatening rain.

'You're not an ordinary man, are you?' The voice of the preacher's wife startled him. She had come up close behind Nylund without him having heard her steps. Maybe it was the blowing wind that covered the sound.

'That depends on what you consider to be ordinary.' Nylund turned the question back on her. 'If breathing, thinking and feeling makes me ordinary, then yes, I am.'

'Let me rephrase that into a suggestion that you are not an ordinary passenger.' She smiled to cover her embarrassment, showing more humility than her husband.

'I'm making a journey. Why isn't that ordinary?' he asked.

'I sense that you're being deliberately evasive, Mr...?'

'Nylund,' he filled in for her.

'... which makes me even more certain that my suspicions are correct,' the woman told him.

'Why am I the subject of such interest?' Nylund was intrigued. 'I thought your husband considered me to be a sinner.'

'My husband doesn't control my thoughts,' was her reply. 'You still haven't given me an answer.'

'With the greatest of respect, ma'am, I don't intend to.' Nylund politely told her she would learn nothing more of him. He wasn't confident that the preacher's wife was asking for her own interest or had been sent by her husband. Nylund suspected it was the latter.

'Very well.' Her voice was curt, a sharp contrast to her earlier manner, which had bordered on sweetness.

Back on the stagecoach and with the journey recommencing, the other passengers fell asleep one by one, with only Nylund remaining awake. A strange feeling came to him as they travelled through the night. Employed to safeguard the stage against robbery, he also felt protective towards his fellow passengers. Maybe he was experiencing a natural emotion; it was at least one he had never felt before. Then perhaps that was because he'd never found himself in such a situation before.

On through the darkness they went, the moon now completely hidden by dark cloud, Nylund constantly aware of the cargo of gold that travelled with them. Like a moth to light, it would surely attract ambushers. In a way he envied the ignorance of his fellow passengers; none of them were aware of what could happen over the next few hours or days. Even if they had the slightest suspicion that all was not right, none had aired it so far. The preacher's wife had sensed something was not as it should be, but her suspicions were of Nylund, not the journey. Nylund himself was painfully aware of what was to come. For him there would be no surprises. It was a mixture of confidence in himself and his own capabilities, combined with a forced lack of imagination that kept Nylund from both worrying, and from thinking of the possibilities that lay ahead. One day, he knew, he would meet somebody faster; somebody smarter; somebody meaner. Maybe that time was today, or next month, or next year; he didn't know and was not prepared to dwell on it, not through fear, but because it cluttered his mind unnecessarily. Nylund had conditioned himself to live fully in the present, and wasn't given much to thinking of the future.

'What are you watching for, mister?' The boy beside him had woken, to notice Nylund looking out into the night.

'Nothing,' Nylund told him, wondering if the boy could detect he was lying. 'Nothing at all.'

'Oh,' the boy replied sleepily, satisfied his question had been answered.

In the darkness of the prairie night Nylund was sure that he had seen the flickering light of a flaming torch, burning brightly. Then, as quickly as it had appeared, it vanished. Nylund breathed deeply, letting the tension leave his muscles; his instinctive reaction had been to tense his body so tightly that pain shot through his arms and legs, almost paralysing him.

Wishing now he could give himself the same reassurance he had afforded the boy, Nylund strained his eyes as he looked out into the blackness, hoping that the flickering flame had existed only in his mind. When it came again, this time much closer to the stagecoach, Nylund knew it was no figment of the imagination. Then a second flaming torch appeared, and a third, a fourth, a fifth, each following along behind the other, closing in on the coach all the time. The driver, too, had seen them, for there was a noticeable lurch as he speeded up the team.

There was the report of a rifle shot. It took Nylund a second to locate its origin. It had come from above him, from the roof of the stage. A second crack followed. The sleeping passengers had been disturbed by the first, and were fully awoken by the next.

'What's happening?' the preacher asked in a demanding way. The third report of the rifle came as he spoke.

'I think we're being attacked.'

Though he was in no doubt as to what was happening, Nylund thought it necessary to be careful in what he said, so as not to alarm the others more than they already were.

'Good Lord! There must be half a dozen of them!' the attorney gasped as he looked out into the dark desert. The flaming torches were so close now that they lit up the faces of the riders who carried them.

A solid blow to the chin was what the lawyer needed right now thought Nylund; having put himself out not to increase the tension of the moment, within a second the attorney had turned the stagecoach into a near uproar. All were in various states of panic.

'And there's two more on the other side!' the attorney shouted, leaning across his wife to look out of the other side of the coach.

At least Nylund could be grateful for that information. Up to now he'd had no idea how many were on the other side, his seating position having prevented him from seeing.

The firing from the stagecoach was continuing, but was now also drawing inaccurate return fire. Until the attackers got much closer, those in the coach were in no danger from the revolver shots. Their gunfire was only meant to alarm, and it had achieved this quickly.

The preacher, muttering prayers, was

busily trying to hide the little money he had, while his wife copied his actions. Across from Nylund, the attorney was slipping his timepiece and chain into the side of his boot, having learnt his lesson once before. Nylund rested his hand on the still-holstered Colt .45. He would use it when they came close enough to allow him to. At present he didn't want to waste his shots or give his position away, as he had the element of surprise on his side, which, outnumbered as Nylund was, was his only advantage.

'Why doesn't the driver stop the stage?' the preacher's wife asked, her question not directed at anyone in particular. 'They only want our valuables; is that worth risking our lives for?'

No one answered; Nylund didn't explain to her that it was the cargo of gold that the bandits were after, not the few trinkets of the passengers. If he did tell her, Nylund wasn't sure whether it would ease her worry or make her worse.

The stagecoach was slowing, the driver

had realized there was no point in trying to outrun his pursuers. They were determined men who wouldn't give up easily. Reining the team in, he slowly stopped the stage, resigned to the fate that had befallen them.

With the wheels only having just stopped turning, the door was opened.

'Everybody out here,' a male voice ordered. A man stepped back from the door, a revolver in his hand, adding: 'Now.'

Quickly, the passengers left the stage, the attorney leading, and Nylund coming last. This time there was no indecision, they had become practised.

The man, who wore no neckerchief to cover his face, demanded they move away from the coach. Which, as one, they did.

Twenty feet away from the stage they stood, with just one man standing guard over them. The others split up to carry out various tasks; four were up on the stage-coach roof, tossing luggage and trunks down onto the ground, which burst open as they landed, spewing their contents out onto the dirty earth. They knew what they were looking for, they knew it was aboard.

'Bill, we've got it!' one of the four called down to a man, obviously their leader, who stood near the team.

'Come on.' He waved them down. 'Let's go.'

The men climbed down, while the leader nodded his head to a small man standing nearby. This had the small man quickly set about unhitching the team, then freeing each horse before sending the animals stampeding off into the night with one shot from his sixgun into the air.

'The horses!' the pretty wife of the attorney gasped. She looked to her husband for an answer. 'What's happening?'

Nylund brought a finger up to his lips. She understood and remained silent. He knew himself what was happening, and it came as no surprise when a blazing torch was thrown into the passenger compartment of the stage. The yellow flames licked at the coach, quickly taking hold and, before their eyes, it was swiftly destroyed.

Nylund was grateful that at least they meant no harm to the passengers – not direct harm, anyway; burning the stagecoach and chasing off the team of horses wasn't beneficial to them, but it showed they weren't going to kill the passengers. That was as long as they didn't present any problems. Nylund wished he could be sure that would be so.

Among the passengers there was confusion and disbelief. Folding his arms across his chest, Nylund hoped the others would take this as a clear signal he wasn't going to make any attempt at being a hero.

'You can't do that!' the attorney exploded, his anger causing the outburst and making him forget his fear.

'I do what I like!' the man snapped back, bringing his ugly face up close to the lawyer's. 'Or do you want to try and stop me?'

To Nylund's astonishment, the attorney pulled himself up to his full height. Maybe, he wondered, the man had reached his breaking point. Responding to the robber's challenge was – in Nylund's opinion – a serious mistake. Anyone could tell the man who held the gun wasn't mentally stable, the staring look of his eyes clearly showed that.

For a few seconds they locked glares before the attorney backed down. A huge grin crossed the robber's face; he was aware he had won their battle.

The little respect that was building in Nylund for the attorney's attempt to find a backbone quickly disappeared as the lawyer changed rapidly from a hero to a coward. The way in which the attorney stood, almost cowering, told the threatening man with the gun that the attorney was subservient to him.

'Jack, come on.'

The other man had mounted up; the strong-box being carried between two of them. The leader called out once more to the single man who stood guard over the passengers.

'Come on, Jack.'

The man started to back away, a noticeable hesitancy in his step, and an expression on his face that warned Nylund. With his eyes flickering between the man's face and gun, Nylund had only a split-second chance to shout a warning. Simultaneously, it seemed, the bandit's revolver barked a shot and with a cry the attorney fell to the ground.

Swinging round to Nylund, the man pointed the revolver at him. With his fingers itching to go for his own holstered Colt, Nylund was aware that the bandit respected him. He would not be shot like some dog. He didn't have a one in a thousand chance of saving himself from the other man's bullet, but would have the opportunity to do some damage.

Riding across to them came the man Nylund assumed to be their leader. It took only one sharp look from the robber on horseback to bring the gun-toting man back into line.

Wheeling the horse around, the desperado rode away. Once they were all on horseback, they rode off, leaving the burning stage-coach behind, lighting up the night sky with its red glow.

FIVE

'Why didn't you do something?' the attorney demanded, clutching his bleeding left arm with his right hand. He had, with his wife's help, struggled up from the ground and onto his knees. 'Instead of standing there uselessly.'

'And what would you have me do?' asked Nylund, hoping he would lead the lawyer into a trap, where he would have to contradict his earlier statement.

'You were prepared to kill one man because he merely tried to steal our valuables.' The attorney's voice was full of anger. 'Yet you let them chase off the horses and burn the stagecoach to the ground. Do you see the logic in that? I certainly don't.'

'I'm just about tired of you, Mr City Attorney,' Nylund stormed, taking a step toward the man.

The attorney turned his body so that his injured arm faced Nylund. This was his form of defence against physical attack. He was confident Nylund wouldn't hit a man who was unable to fight back.

'You shot one man, yet let another try to kill me.'

'I understand now,' Nylund sarcastically exclaimed. 'You wanted me to kill him.'

'What stopped you? Surely he would be just one more notch on your gun.'

Nylund chuckled, he couldn't take what the man said seriously, and that annoyed the attorney. There was a sharp intake of breath from the lawyer as Nylund drew his revolver. The colour drained from his cheeks as he looked down the barrel of the Colt.

'You wanted me to shoot him with this?'

'Yes.' The attorney gulped nervously.

'Then say I did that,' Nylund continued, 'and his friends began to shoot at us. Now, this is only a six-shooter. Having regard to the fact there were eight of them, how many of us do you think would still be alive after I'd shot all them? That's if I was able to gun down six, and reload before they killed me.'

Twirling the Colt around in his hand Nylund put it back into the holster, and walked away from the small group to the burning stage, where he kicked dust over the flames in an attempt to extinguish the fire and save the little that was left of the construction.

Nylund could sense someone standing beside him, and he turned to see the attorney's wife sifting through her luggage, which was strewn across the ground.

'The preacher said we need a bandage for my husband's arm,' she explained to Nylund without looking up at him. 'I'll find something in here that will make do.'

Unable to put out the fire, Nylund had to give up his attempt, and stood back to let it burn. There was no point in trying to save it now, the main structure had been destroyed already, and the remainder would be no use to anyone.

'Do you think this will do?' She held a bundle of ruffled material up to Nylund. 'Is this all right for a bandage?'

'You'll need to cut it into strips,' Nylund explained, pulling his knife from the pouch on his belt. 'Let me do it for you.'

Kneeling down beside the woman, Nylund ran the knife along the material, cutting it into thick strips.

'My husband doesn't mean any harm,' she apologized. 'Occasionally he speaks before he has had time to think. I know that he later regrets what he says, but is too proud to take it back.'

'That should be enough,' Nylund told her as he slit the last part of the material, its softness under his fingers telling him it was an item of her clothing.

'Thank you,' she said quietly, taking the makeshift bandage from him to return to her wounded husband's side.

'Praise the Lord, the bullet didn't enter his arm,' the preacher told Nylund as he came to look at the attorney's injury.

'It's little more than a graze,' Nylund commented off-handedly. 'The bleeding makes it look worse than it really is.'

The lawyer looked up at Nylund, expecting some sympathy but not receiving any. Having seen men with limbs blown off, and little of their faces left, Nylund could not sympathize with the superficially wounded attorney.

Nylund watched as the preacher removed the attorney's coat, then tore open the sleeve of his shirt to examine the wound more closely, making use of the light from the burning stage. He began to remove the cap of a water-bottle, puzzling Nylund as to how he had come by it.

'Go easy with that water,' Nylund warned him. 'Don't waste any.'

'I've got to clean the wound,' snapped the preacher.

'And we've got to survive in this desert until we reach help, or help reaches us,' Nylund quickly returned. 'Conserving water is the most important thing we can do.'

'I'm not risking the wound becoming infected.' The attorney's selfishness came through.

'And I'm not putting six lives at risk for the sake of one,' replied Nylund, directing his words at the lawyer.

'Since when did you take charge?' asked the lawyer sarcastically, his pain briefly forgotten.

'It's obvious somebody has to take control.'

'Then why not me?' The attorney smiled in a smug, over-confident manner that annoyed Nylund. 'I'm without doubt the most well-educated person here, apart from the preacher of course, yet he's probably a little too senior in years to want to take charge.'

'Quite right, I'm a follower, not a leader,' the preacher agreed.

'All right, you take charge.'

Nylund's statement had the lawyer raise his eyebrows in surprise. He had imagined Nylund wouldn't give in so easily, if at all.

'Just one thing.' Nylund pointed a finger

to emphasize his words. 'Once you've run out of clean water, where do you intend to get more? Because come sun-up, you're going to see we are stranded right in the middle of an almost barren desert. There's no water within several days' walk.'

With that, Nylund walked away from them. He had said all he needed to; having sown doubt about the attorney's leadership into the minds of the other passengers, he knew that, before long, they would be coming to him, asking him to take charge.

Collecting his bag and bedroll from where they had been thrown from the roof of the stage, Nylund found himself a comfortable place to spend the night. There was nothing anyone could do while darkness prevailed. Come daybreak Nylund would take stock of the situation and decide what action to take, this action pertaining to whether he was thinking just for himself, or for all the passengers. If, and he considered this to be very unlikely, the lawyer was still leading the other passengers in the morning, Nylund would consider how, in the terms of his employment, he would go about recovering the cargo of gold. He knew the odds were well against him; to start with he was one man against eight, and a man on foot against men on horses.

Nylund awoke suddenly, disturbed by footfalls coming towards him. Hand to his holster he drew the Colt. Clutching it tightly he covered the revolver with his coat as he peered through the brightening dawn to see who was walking up on him.

'You're awake, good.' The stage driver spoke to Nylund. The man looked tired and his face was drawn. He'd obviously not slept well.

'What's happening?' Getting to his feet, Nylund put the Colt back into its holster. 'How are the passengers?'

'They're still asleep.' There was hesitancy in the driver's voice. Nylund could sense that he either wanted to tell him something, or ask his advice. 'Bob's gone off to see if he can round up the horses.'

'He should never have gone.' Nylund was immediately critical of the other driver's action. 'The hot sun can be a killer; there's no protection from it.'

'I tried to talk him out of it,' explained the stage driver. 'But he's so headstrong.'

'When did he go?'

'About an hour since.'

Nylund shook his head, it was too long for him to go after the driver. He had no chance of catching up with the man and bringing him back, even if he would listen to Nylund's advice.

'What can we do?' asked the driver, expecting Nylund to have the answer.

'Nothing. We can do nothing.' Nylund knew it wasn't the reply the man wanted, but it was all he was going to get. 'The man made his own decision; whether we think it's the right one or not doesn't matter. He's not here to discuss it with us – we're wasting our time worrying.'

Tying up his bedroll, Nylund was prepared for the day ahead.

‘What water and food have we got?’

‘Very little,’ explained the driver, ‘at least, not much for the eight of us. One small barrel of water, and even less food.’

‘You’re a sensible man,’ said Nylund. ‘You and I both know this land is far from hospitable. That water is, right now, far more valuable to us than gold dust.’

‘I know that,’ agreed the man. ‘Apart from the barrel, I’ve seen the preacher with a couple of water bottles, one of which I think is full.’

‘Good morning.’

As the two men spoke of him, the preacher had come walking toward them, unaware that he was being discussed. The almost bouncy walk of the religious man clearly showed he wasn’t fully aware of the gravity of their situation, seeing it as something of an adventure.

Nylund and the driver nodded in reply to his greeting.

‘Will help be along soon?’ the preacher asked innocently, smiling as he spoke.

‘Help won’t come until someone knows we need it,’ replied Nylund, seeing the man’s face fall. ‘At present it’s only us that knows what’s happened. When we don’t arrive to change the team, then someone is going to know we’ve had problems, but that won’t be for many days.’

‘You mean we have to just stay here and wait?’

‘We can’t stay here,’ Nylund told him. ‘Not when the noon sun arrives. By then we will have to find shade. But, of course, that’s not for me to arrange. For that you’ll have to speak to the man who has taken charge. I think you’ll find the attorney is over that way.’

Turning sharply on his heel the preacher walked away from them, the slight stagger in his walk denoting his earlier cheerfulness had been induced by liquor.

‘You’re not letting that fool of an attorney take charge, are you?’ the driver queried, regarding Nylund as a natural leader. ‘He’s not capable, that’s clear to see.’

‘It’s nothing to do with me.’ Nylund settled his hat on his head. ‘I offered my help, but it was rejected.’

‘We need to stay together.’ The driver spoke wisely. ‘But the lawyer knows nothing of this country. Under his leadership we’re in danger. He could get us killed.’

‘Like I said,’ Nylund repeated. ‘It’s nothing to do with me.’

Swinging his bedroll over his shoulder, he walked away.

SIX

The sun, rising higher in the sky, was getting hotter, bringing discomfort as Nylund walked on, the dry grit getting into his eyes, nostrils and mouth as a gentle breeze grew stronger. With his destination uncertain he carried on. He felt no guilt at having left the others to their fate. They had made their choice, it wasn't up to him to have them change their minds. The men had decided to stay, and, naturally enough, their wives remained with them. The only worry Nylund had was for the boy. It would have been wrong for him to come with Nylund. The prairie was a dangerous place for a man alone, but it was made even more hazardous with the responsibility of a boy. As a group they maybe had a better chance of survival.

As Nylund saw it they either stayed

together, with him taking charge, or he left alone; there was no way he would put his life in the hands of an inept, city-bred lawyer.

With sweat building up on his body, Nylund removed his coat, taking the time to sip from the water-bottle which he always carried with him. Nylund swirled the liquid around his dry mouth before finally swallowing it. The sun was growing hotter all the time, its rays making his skin burn. To keep on walking would dehydrate him even further, something he could not risk. Even though he had consciously made the decision to no longer have any responsibility for the other passengers, his mind kept turning to them, the urge to go back becoming more powerful all the time. But that would be a mistake. He would return to find nothing had changed, with the exception of their water supply having become lower, while at the same time they would be under the misapprehension that he had come back for his own welfare. Certainly, Nylund thought, the attorney would express such an opinion.

No, he had to keep going, this way he had the chance of reaching safety himself, and sending help to them.

The heat was so intense now that Nylund had to stop and rest. To go on in such a temperature would be to court disaster. Ahead of him lay a ridge. Nylund figured that it would possibly afford some shade on the other side. Getting back to his feet, he walked the distance to the ridge, feeling his legs weakening under him as he went. Pausing to take one more sip of water, he cursed himself for being so foolish as to carry on walking when he should have stopped long ago to allow his body to recover.

Rubbing the grit from his eyes with the backs of his hands, Nylund blinked several times, hoping that the image in front of him was no mirage that would disappear when he looked harder. It was still there; a tiny haven in the middle of a vast wilderness. A small wooden shack offering a sanctuary of shade. How it came to be there, and who it belonged to, Nylund didn't know, and right at that moment it wasn't important.

With perspiration rolling down his forehead and his body weary, Nylund managed to run toward the building, dropping his bedroll and bag on the ground as he did so. Half falling, half running, he reached the shack, slamming his body against the door, which flew open! Staggering into the building, he coughed and spluttered as thick dust assailed his nostrils. In three strides, Nylund was at the rear wall, and he slid down it, sitting on the floor, allowing time to get his breath back and let his body cool.

Once he had recovered from his exertions Nylund was able to take in his surroundings. The shack consisted of nothing more than a single room, the interior of which was very dark, illuminated only by the light that came in through the open door. The sole window had been boarded over. Pulling off his boots, Nylund shook out the sandy grit that had been blown into them. He had been walking since just after sun-up. How far he had come he didn't know, but his body felt as if it had been a very long way. Finding shade had been wonderful for him. He had expected, or at least hoped, to find a rock cluster, under which he could crawl to seek relief from the burning sun. The shack was above all his expectations.

When he was fully rested he had a decision to make. It was whether he should go on again and find the help that he had left the others to get, or to return to the passengers and lead them to the shack, where they would be out of harm from the hot sun. To take the first choice could seem like an act of selfishness, but if he went back they would without doubt come to the building; yet would it be too long a walk for the women, and was the elderly preacher up to such a physical task?

With those thoughts on his mind, Nylund fell into an exhausted sleep. It was dark when he awoke, stretching and yawning, unaware he had slept for so long. As his eyes grew accustomed to the darkness, Nylund realized it wasn't nighttime, for a bright light shone through a narrow crack in the boards across the window.

The door was now closed, although Nylund had left it open. Assuming the wind had got stronger and had blown it shut he stood, walking over to the door. Tugging on its handle he found it refused to budge. Thinking it may have stuck, he pulled harder. Still it wouldn't open. It was at this time he began to suspect there was something sinister to the door having closed.

Pulling his boots back on, Nylund drew his Colt. If his being locked in was no accident he wanted to be able to defend himself. Going to the window he tried to find a gap through which he could look out. The narrow crack that allowed light in was too small to let him see out. In the semi-darkness, to which he was now growing accustomed, Nylund searched for a lever with which he could shift the boards across the window. Finding nothing suitable he hacked at the crack with his knife, the strong, sharp blade opening it further, allowing him a slightly better view.

The door was set in the front wall of the building, making the viewing of it impossible from his angle. Having cut away enough of the board to allow him to get a finger-hold, Nylund took a tight grip and pulled. Splinters of wood digging into his skin, and stabbing under his nails, he could feel a tearing pain in the muscles of his forearms as, with all his strength, he tried to pull away the boards. At first they refused to move, then suddenly part of one came away, splitting the board in two. Though the window was still barred, Nylund now had more room in which to manoeuvre his hands, and he prised the boards from the window. Smashing the glass with the butt of his revolver, he cleared the jagged edges from the frame. The sound of the breaking glass seemed louder in the open priarie than it really was.

Nylund wondered if he wasn't becoming paranoid, for his action in breaking the glass had attracted no attention, nor drawn any gunfire, as he had half expected. As he cautiously looked outside, he could see nothing out of the ordinary. Raising himself up onto his toes he could see the outside of the door; the latch was down, preventing it from opening. Going to the inside of the door he discovered the mechanism that worked the latch from the interior had broken off.

Grabbing either side of the frame, Nylund pulled his knees up to his chest and launched himself out of the window, landing on the ground with a thump, springing on the balls of his feet to absorb the impact. Feeling something of a fool at having accidentally locked himself in the shack, Nylund lifted the latch on the door. Forcing the blade of his knife behind it he levered it away from the wood, ensuring that the door could never be locked again.

With the main heat of the day over, Nylund didn't find it too uncomfortable to explore the exterior of the cabin. On closer examination it proved to be of a sturdier construction than he had first thought. He was sure that whatever the weather outside, the interior of the cabin would be impervious to it. The building was many years old, he could tell that from the signs of wear. To his surprise he found a well at the rear of the small building. Expecting it to be dry, Nylund picked up a small rock and dropped it into the well's mouth. There was a lengthy silence, during which time Nylund thought the stone must have hit the bottom of the well, so he picked up another rock, larger than the first, letting it fall from his fingers just as he heard the first stone splash into water.

Nylund searched for some means with which he could reach the water. He found a length of rope not far from the well. Frayed and brittle from lying in the sun, the rope was stiff. Wrapping it around his knuckles, Nylund pulled on the rope, satisfying himself that it was strong enough for the task. A second search revealed a tin bucket, the handle of which was still intact. With some difficulty Nylund wrapped one end of the rope around the handle, tying a knot to secure it, the roughness of the rope scratching his fingers. Back at the well he slowly lowered the bucket and rope into the seemingly bottomless hole. Aware the well would have needed to have been dug deep in this landscape, Nylund admired the men who had constructed it, for doubtless it had been hard work. Stopping occasionally to pull in the rope to feel if he had reached the water, Nylund continued to lower. He tugged the rope. This time there was weight on the other end.

Hand over hand, Nylund heaved the bucket back up, its heaviness evincing that it was full, if not quite to the brim then almost with water. Thankful now that he had tied such a tight knot when attaching the rope to the bucket, Nylund heaved. He hadn't realized the toll his long walk in the hot sun had taken on his body, and he needed to take an occasional rest.

The bucket came within Nylund's view, the sight of the cool, clear water inspiring him to pull harder and faster. As he got it near to the mouth of the well the strength in his arms gave way, and the rope slipped through his fingers. The bucket crashed against the sides, spilling the liquid contents for which Nylund was so desirous, falling several feet down the well until he was able to check the rope. With it still slipping through his fingers Nylund was able to slow its descent, then stop it completely. He had lost about twenty feet, and again began to pull it up, his hands aching where the frayed, brittle rope had scraped the skin from his palms, drawing blood.

Wrapping the rope around his lower left arm, Nylund reached into the well, grabbed the bucket's handle, and in one swift movement lifted it over the wall of the well and down onto the ground beside him. About a quarter of its contents had been lost when the bucket fell, but it left more than enough water to satisfy Nylund's needs. Pulling his shirt up over his head, he threw it onto the ground. Picking the bucket up he tipped it over his head, drinking the cold clear water as it ran over his mouth. Coursing over his shoulders, down his back and chest, the water envigorated him, his hot, dry skin stinging pleasantly as the water made contact.

The decision as to whether to go back for the other passengers had now been taken from Nylund's hands. With shade and clear drinking water available, he had no choice but to go back and lead them here. Not to do so would be selfish in the extreme. Nylund dropped the bucket into the well for a second time, pulling it back up full. Going back into the shack he retrieved his water bottle, filling it from the bucket. Drinking from the bucket, his thirst already quenched, Nylund wanted to more than satisfy himself; the extra water, he hoped, would be an insurance against his thirst growing severe again.

Nylund considered it best to return immediately to where the burnt-out stage was. It was the cooler part of the day, and when night fell he would be able to walk in comfort, with moonlight to show him his way. His quick return would also prevent any further suffering for the other passengers. He was sure that they would still be where he had left them. Under the attorney's leadership he couldn't see them going anywhere.

Hunger was now the only problem facing Nylund. He had found water and shade, but food would be more difficult to come by. In his bag he had bread, but had chosen to save that for a time when his hunger became too difficult to bear. When he had previously considered his situation, and that of the others, Nylund had believed that lack of fresh water would be the point around which their survival would revolve, but now he had to think differently. Food had become the priority. But where that could be obtained in this wilderness of a prairie he didn't know. The little that grew and thrived in such a place was either spiky or poisonous.

Leaving his bedroll and bag in the shack,

Nylund threw his coat over a shoulder, having allowed the sun to dry out his shirt when he had put it back on after washing his body. Hat on head, Nylund shut the door of the shack as best he could, for since he had removed the latch it no longer shut flush.

Walking away from the building he began to retrace his footsteps on the long journey back to the other passengers. Now, with a destination firmly in his mind, Nylund walked with a determination he had not possessed on the previous trip. An inherent sense of direction kept him on the right path, and he recognized the small landmarks, unnoticeable to most people, that he had seen when passing this way before; a collection of rocks, none bigger than his hand, that lay in a natural circle, and a small ridge of sand built by the wind.

As the day became a cool evening, and then a cold night, Nylund pulled on his coat, appreciating its warmth. For hours he trudged on, not stopping once for even a minute's rest. He felt he had to put the other passengers' safety before his own comfort. He had drunk cool water and taken a sleep in the shade; they, on the other hand, had not had the chance to participate in either of these luxuries. Nylund wouldn't rest until he knew they were safe, and were on the way to the shack with him.

Nylund carried on walking through the night, his mind forcing him to go on while his body wanted him to stop. Eventually he had to give way to his physical needs, and he took a brief rest, freshening his mouth with water from his bottle as he did so.

Though not wanting to admit it to himself he was aware that a character flaw in his own personality made him eager to return and announce his success to the others. He felt he was showing how capable he was compared to the inadequacy of the attorney. Even in this situation, where life and death could hinge on his actions, Nylund knew he was being childish yet was unable to rid himself of the feeling.

Back on his feet again, the short rest was

as good as several hours to Nylund, and his body felt fifty per cent stronger. The grit had again blown into Nylund's boots, but now, as he was no longer walking aimlessly, it didn't bother him as much as before.

Nylund speeded up almost to a run as he recognized landmarks, a large rock formation to his left, and a much smaller one to his right. The area in which he and the passengers had spent the previous night was not far ahead. On the air he could smell the faint smoke from the burnt-out stage.

As he grew closer the moonlight lit the scene for him. The remains of the stagecoach lay on the barren ground, the few metal pieces of the construction glinting amid the black ashes.

Nylund stopped dead in his tracks. He felt as if he had run into a wall, such was the shock he received. There was no point in him going further. His eyes scoured the area. He could see for a long way and, no matter how hard he looked, the passengers were nowhere to be seen.

SEVEN

Nylund shook his head in disbelief. Less than twelve hours ago he had walked away from here, leaving the other passengers behind him. Over and over in his mind Nylund considered the possibilities of where they could have gone. Had another stage come along? No, he had to dismiss that, there wasn't a stage due to pass by. Nylund decided that he had to forget all thoughts of rescue, which left him with one clear and worrying thought – that those who had ambushed and robbed the stage had returned.

There were enough reasons why they should do so. Maybe they had got worried and returned to ensure that they left no witnesses, or they had got greedy, wanting more than the gold. They could have come back to take what little valuables the passengers had. Whatever, that didn't explain the disappearance of the passengers. Nylund thought, his stomach churning as he did so, that at least there would be bodies. He could feel a little happier that there were no corpses, but he was still left with a mystery.

Though the moon was clear it was still too dark for Nylund to be able to search for tracks. He would have to wait for sun-up in a couple of hours time. Until then there was little for him to do. Kicking through the ashes of the stage, he found a few remaining burning embers. Choosing a comfortable place to sit, Nylund waited for daybreak, his busy mind not allowing him the chance to rest.

When sun-up finally came he had exhausted every avenue of possibility, almost driving himself crazy in the process. If the worst had happened, Nylund would feel guilty and blame himself. Yet he couldn't have foreseen what would happen. Had he been able to, he would never have left them. Apart from the stage driver's rifle, he didn't know whether they had any weapons. They weren't exactly defenceless, yet neither were they well protected. Using caution to make sure he wasn't rushing headlong into an ambush, Nylund returned to the spot where he had last seen the passengers. The ground was disturbed, scuffed by feet and showing signs of recent occupation. Dropping to his knees, he was able to find the beginning of a track leading away from the area. Nylund was able to follow the trail of man or beast over most terrain and he swiftly caught onto the trail of the passengers. So spread out were their footprints that Nylund was able to establish that there were only six people. Obviously the driver, who had gone looking for the horses, had been unsuccessful, and had not returned to the others.

The dry, soft gritty ground made the trail easy to follow, and Nylund found himself almost at a running pace as he followed it, needing to check it only infrequently. The ground was flat and Nylund could see for a long distance. His eye was caught by a scattered collection of dots ahead of him. Though they were too far ahead to distinguish, Nylund was confident it was the other passengers. At least now his worries could be eased as nothing serious had happened to them. Nothing serious that was, until now. Nylund was so glad he had returned, for they were now walking further into the prairie, and away from any possible help.

Through guesswork he assumed they had begun to walk shortly after he had left the shack to return to them. Fortunately the women and the elderly preacher had slowed them, which would allow Nylund to catch up quickly. With them within his view he was filled with energy, and began to run at speed after them. This proved to be a mistake in the growing morning heat and he rapidly became tired, having to stop to prevent the tiredness turning to exhaustion. He had to attract their attention. At present they were slowly increasing the distance between them and him. Snatching his Colt from its holster Nylund fired into the air, letting all six shots go, one after another.

With some relief he saw that his action had been effective. Not only had they stopped, but they were coming back toward him. Taking another swill of water, Nylund steeled himself and walked to meet them, the plain, unchanging desert making the walk seem longer than it really was.

As the five passengers and driver came near he could see that they all looked tired, the two women especially. The clothes of each of them were caked with sand, and their skin, where exposed, was burnt red.

'I didn't think we'd see you again.' The attorney spoke with sarcasm in his voice.

'If you'd kept on walking that way you certainly wouldn't have,' Nylund returned with a snipe of his own. 'All you're going to find that way is prairie and more prairie.'

'So why have you come to join us?' smiled the attorney cleverly, believing Nylund was only trying to destroy his credibility.

'I've not come to join you,' Nylund returned, 'but to lead you to shade and water.'

'You've reached help?' the driver asked, stepping forward eagerly.

'No. But I've found shade and a deep well of clear water.'

'We're darn near out of water,' the stage driver told Nylund. 'We've only one full bottle left.' He nodded at the attorney. 'And he's got that.'

'How far away is the well?' the pretty wife of the attorney asked.

'About a day's walk away, ma'am,' Nylund replied with a smile. After being alone in the vast prairie the beautiful woman was a joy to behold. 'Yet it could be further. You've come some distance this way, we need to go back.'

'We've come this far for nothing?' the preacher stormed, his anger directed more at Nylund than the attorney, the man who had brought them further into the wilderness. 'My wife is near to collapse.'

'Not only have you come this way for nothing, you've also risked your lives in doing so.' Nylund wasn't intentionally meaning to wound the lawyer, but knew he had done so, for the attorney's face was turning crimson with rage, deepening the colour of his already burnt skin. 'Come with me, now. I've found a small shack where you can rest in shade, and also a source of water.'

'And what about being rescued?' the attorney fumed. 'Do you intend we sit in this sanctuary of yours waiting for help to pass by?'

'I intend to get these people out of this sun and get these ladies to safety. Our priority has to be to stay alive.' Nylund wasn't speaking through emotion, but with common sense.

'Then lead us to it.' Forgetting his anger, the preacher, his hand holding the arm of his wife, helping the woman stay upright, stepped forward.

As a group the others came forward, gathering around Nylund as if he were a shepherd and they his flock. They were the weak prepared to be led by the strong.

'Wait,' the lawyer called, standing alone. 'Why are you going with him?'

'Because he will lead us to shade and water,' the driver snapped, annoyed by the lawyer's delaying.

'I was leading you out of here.'

'You were leading them nowhere but into danger,' Nylund corrected him, secretly wondering if the attorney actually believed the nonsense he was speaking.

Turning his body partly away from them, the attorney walked slowly back in the direction they had previously been heading.

'You followed me once,' he told the group. 'Now do it again.'

'Don't be foolish, man.' Nylund gave the lawyer the benefit of the doubt, maybe the hot sun had driven the city man a little crazy.

The attorney halted, making Nylund think he had seen sense.

'Who is coming with me?' the lawyer wanted to know. 'And who is going with him?'

'This isn't about taking sides.' Nylund was losing patience with the man. 'We're wasting time.'

Nylund walked away, gaining personal satisfaction in that all but the attorney came with him.

'Daphne, I forbid you to go!' Shouting at his wife, the attorney caused her to halt.

Putting out his hand to stop the woman going to her husband, Nylund spoke sternly to her.

'Go with him and you'll certainly go to your death.'

'He's my husband,' the pretty woman told him, her voice so low that Nylund could only just hear her. 'I have to go.'

'Come with us, please,' Nylund spoke gently to her. 'For your own sake you must.'

'Daphne, come here.'

'I have to go.' While she said one thing, her eyes said another.

'Please, think what you're doing.' The preacher let his voice be heard. 'This man has found us water. Please try and convince your husband to come with us.'

'He's so...' She left her sentence unfinished.

'Get back from her, preacher!' the attorney shouted. From the inside of his coat he pulled out a derringer, waving it threateningly.

Seeing the crazed look in the lawyer's eyes, the preacher did the wisest thing, which was to step back.

At this, Nylund realized he had to become involved, and drew the Colt .45 from its holster.

'Let us be sensible,' Nylund suggested. 'You put the gun away and we can return to talking.'

The confidence the attorney had briefly experienced with the derringer in his hand drained away as he saw Nylund draw the Colt. For whatever reason, the attorney had become obsessed with the route he was taking. From Nylund's understanding the man was following nothing more than a hunch, as he had no knowledge whatsoever of the prairie's terrain.

The lawyer's wife shot a terrified look at Nylund, reminding him of a cornered animal too small and weak to be able to defend itself.

Fortunately the lawyer had retained some glimmer of intelligence, and, staring hard at the Colt, dropped the derringer to the ground. With a giant leap Nylund was in front of him, grabbing the weapon from the dirt. As he straightened, Nylund brought up a clenched fist, catching the lawyer under the chin. Following the first punch with a second to the stomach, he sent the man sprawling onto the ground.

A minute ago the woman had been terrified of her husband. Now she was at his side, dabbing at the blood that was running from his mouth with a dainty handkerchief. Having been belittled by Nylund, the attorney searched for a way in which to recover his self-esteem.

'Why didn't you shoot me? That's your answer, isn't it? Why don't you go ahead now and do it?' He sniggered. 'I'm unarmed, that'll make it easier for you.'

Nylund didn't speak. Cocking the weapon

he held it out, aiming its barrel at the attorney's chest, and pulled the trigger. It fell on an empty chamber.

'Lord, stop him!' the preacher cried out.

'There's no need for His intervention,' explained Nylund. 'All the chambers are empty. I haven't reloaded since I fired all six shots to attract your attention.'

'You faced a man threatening you with a weapon while your own revolver was unloaded?' The preacher shook his head in disbelief. 'You are certainly a man of immense courage.'

'Maybe I'm just a fool.' Nylund laughed off the compliment. 'Whatever, this sun is getting hot, and I'm getting thirsty, as I'm sure you all are. Let's be on our way.'

This time there was no disagreement. Though he followed them, the attorney did so reluctantly, at a distance. With the two women and the preacher the pace was naturally slow, and Nylund felt his first estimation of a day's walk was inaccurate; he guessed it would take much longer. Their delay in starting out had set their journey time back considerably.

When the noon sun was high in the sky, Nylund would have suggested they stop and rest, since it was the hottest part of the day, but he saw it as essential that they carry on. That way they would reach the shack much quicker.

'My wife really needs to rest,' the preacher called to Nylund, who stopped and walked back to where the woman was just barely able to walk, forcing one foot in front of the other.

'I'm sorry, we can't stop.' Nylund was sincere in his apology. He spoke to the religious man's wife. 'Would a sip of water help?'

'Please,' she nodded, her voice weak. Nylund handed her his water-bottle, letting her drink as much as she needed. There was no need now to be conservative.

With her severe thirst she drank deeply, leaving only a little remaining in the bottle. Apologetically, she handed it back to Nylund. Refreshed now, she walked on with an extra spring to her step.

'How are you feeling?' Nylund slowed to speak to the attorney's wife, the attorney himself walking several paces behind her. 'Are you able to keep up?'

'It's difficult,' she answered. 'It's so hot.'

'It'll get cooler soon,' Nylund assured her, aware that it was little comfort at the moment. 'If you want water, let me know.'

'That's all right, my husband...' she began, stopped, then with embarrassment finished her sentence, '...has a water-bottle.'

Nylund smiled, there was no need to say anything. He turned back to look at the attorney, who, head slightly bowed, was following along completely remote from the others.

'He had that coming,' the stage driver told Nylund, nodding toward the attorney. 'Ever since you left he's been throwing his weight around, telling us rather than asking us what we should do. There was no arguing with him. None of us wanted to be alone, so we joined in with what he suggested, thinking there was safety in numbers.'

'I only wish I hadn't had to do it,' confessed Nylund.

'You probably saved his life with your action.'

'Yes. But that still doesn't make me feel any better,' Nylund said, then became silent.

'Help me. Help!' The preacher's voice broke the silence.

Both Nylund and the driver ran to the religious man, discovering his wife lying on the ground. The heat too much for her, she had collapsed. Gently Nylund trickled water from his bottle over her face, its freshness bringing her round.

'You must think me such a fool,' she apologized.

'Of course we don't,' Nylund replied. 'You've walked a long way. But we have further to go.'

'You can't expect my wife to go any further.' The preacher caught Nylund's arm in a tight grip. 'She's not strong enough to go on.'

‘I’m not suggesting she walks,’ Nylund told the elderly man, sweeping the woman up off the ground and into his arms. ‘I’ll carry her.’

‘You can’t,’ the preacher protested vainly, his worry being for Nylund. ‘You’re weak yourself.’

‘The sooner we get there, the better it’ll be for all of us,’ he told him, and began to walk again.

EIGHT

Nylund was getting desperately tired, his arms were aching with pain. The preacher's wife wasn't too heavy, but after having walked for so long carrying her it was becoming a strain. Every step was becoming difficult. There wasn't that much further go; knowing that helped him carry on.

'Look at me, a silly old woman, having to be carried.' The preacher's wife laughed in embarrassment, her movement putting further strain on Nylund's arms.

'Let me take her for a while,' the driver offered. 'You must be tired.'

'We'll soon be there.' Nylund refused his offer. The stage driver was only slightly built, and in all honesty, Nylund figured the preacher's wife would have an easier time carrying him than he her.

Up ahead Nylund could see the ridge that had led to his discovery of the shack, and knew that within the hour they would all be in shade.

'Once we're over the ridge it'll be ahead of us,' he told the others, happy now that he could confidently tell them where the shack was, as opposed to his earlier non-committal 'not much further'.

The passengers were straggled out behind him according to age and fitness. First came the driver, his light build and daily physical work enabling him to keep nearly in line with Nylund. Then followed the boy; though overweight his youthfulness allowed him to keep up. The attorney's wife walked a little ahead of the preacher, and last came the attorney. With neither age nor physical impairments to slow him he chose to walk separately from the rest.

There were gasps and shouts of delight from the passengers as the building came into view. Nylund had begun to believe that a couple of the passengers, notably the lawyer and the preacher, had begun to suspect that the shack was nothing more substantial than a figment of his imagination.

As when Nylund had approached the cabin before, his pace speeded up, along with that of the others. Physical tiredness and mental weariness were pushed aside as they forced themselves on; even the attorney was breaking into a hurried pace.

They gathered around the front door. Despite having come so far they were reluctant to enter. Whether they were respecting the rights of the property owner and felt it wrong to intrude, or just couldn't believe they had arrived, wasn't quite clear.

With the woman still in his arms, Nylund used a foot to kick the door open, stepping through the doorway in time to catch the reverberating door with his shoulder. The building wasn't as dusty now as it had been when Nylund first arrived. The broken window had filled the single room with fresher air, a gentle breeze removing the thicker dust. Putting the preacher's wife down onto her feet at the far wall of the shack, where he knew it to be cooler, Nylund steadied her as she tottered, struggling to regain the use of her legs.

Nylund moved to get his bedroll for her to sit on. His hand reached out to where he had left it, only to find his fingers closing on air. Looking down, Nylund found it wasn't there. He spun round, his eyes scouring the room. On the old table which dominated the small shack was his bedroll. At first Nylund was bewildered. How had it got there? Surely he hadn't put it there. Or was he getting confused? It had been a strange time when he left the building to return to the others. A mixture of euphoria and relief could have led him to do something he had forgotten. Not telling any of the others of his confusion, Nylund gave the preacher's wife the bedroll on which to rest, then led the passengers out to the well.

Lowering the bucket into the well once more, Nylund ignored the scratch of the rope on his palms, opening up the earlier injuries.

‘Ladies, first,’ Nylund said, filling the water-bottle for the preacher to take into his wife, and allowing the attorney’s wife to drink before her husband, the stage driver, or the boy.

When the preacher came out to the well Nylund had to fill the bucket again. The old man drank and drank, his thirst apparently worse that that of the others.

There was a niggling doubt in Nylund’s mind as they went back into the shade of the shack, the passengers content to either sit or lie as they fell asleep. He was nearly a hundred per cent certain he had not left the bedroll on the table, although it was impossible to prove otherwise, and really there was no other explanation than that he had put it there. Sitting himself down on the floor inside the door, Nylund reloaded his Colt. He had a sense of insecurity with it empty.

‘I’m really hungry, mister.’ The boy spoke to Nylund from across the room. ‘We ate all that was on the stage, but I got pains now. I’m really hungry.’

'I've some bread in my bag,' Nylund told him. He didn't like to see the boy in discomfort, but he'd not give him all the bread, just enough to take the edge off his hunger.

Where had he left his bag? It felt strange to him, having to account for his own actions, yet they seemed to be those of another person. Walking around the room, gently stepping over the bodies of the sleeping passengers so as not to wake them, he searched for the bag. As if he was playing some sort of game with himself, Nylund felt he was the loser, for nowhere could he find it. The bag had disappeared. Since there was nowhere else it could be inside the building, Nylund went outside, the boy following him.

After searching along the front of the building, Nylund went to the rear and followed his earlier route to the well; he had not wandered further, nor strayed from the path.

'Is this what you're looking for?' the boy asked, holding the bag out to Nylund and able to manage a smile, despite his hunger. 'Couldn't you remember where you left it?'

'No.' Nylund forced himself to join in with the boy's amusement. Not wanting to alarm the youngster, he asked, in a matter of interest way: 'Where did you find it?'

'Over there, at the back of the building, beside that lean-to.' The boy pointed.

Until that moment Nylund hadn't been aware of the lean-to's existence, and beyond a doubt he had never put the bag there. Taking out the bread Nylund broke it in two, handing the boy one part, and returning the other to his bag. The youngster ate it ravenously.

Nylund was very disturbed by the thought that there was a stranger hiding close by. He had immediately dismissed the idea of an animal, which wasn't even probable. Though wanting to alert the others to the presence, neither did he wish to alarm them, but he needed them to be on their guard. Avoiding making an announcement to all of them, Nylund roused the stage driver from his slumber. Leading him outside, Nylund told him of his discoveries.

'Who do you think it is? Are there more than one? Is there any danger?'

Nylund raised his hands to stop the man from speaking further.

'I know no more than I've told you.' Nylund prevented any further talk. 'You've still got the rifle?'

'Yes, it's inside.'

'Keep it by you always, and take this.' Nylund pulled the derringer from inside his coat. 'If anything should happen, give this back to the attorney.'

'Why are you doing this?' the driver asked Nylund. 'Where are you going?'

'We need food and we need help,' Nylund explained to him. 'I'm going to do my best to find both.'

'Let me come with you.'

'No. Thank you. But it's best you stay here. You're the only one that can handle a weapon.'

'If you're sure?'

'Yes,' Nylund nodded. Not only did he not want the man along to slow him down, he would feel happier knowing that the passengers had some protection, with the driver standing guard.

'When will you be going?'

'Not for a couple of hours.' Nylund was tired, and he needed to catch up on some rest. Once he set out again there was no knowing when his next opportunity to sleep would come. Nylund was going to snatch the chance while he had it.

'Mister, mister, come look!' Shouting loudly, the boy came running from the shack and around to the well.

'What is it?' Nylund asked, trying not to respond to the boy's excitement. 'What's wrong?'

'There's something happening out on the prairie,' the boy shouted, waving his arms.

Seeing the stage driver's hand tighten on the derringer, Nylund knew he had made a wise choice in selecting him from the others to stand guard. The man displayed an alertness he liked. Where another man might have considered hiding back in the building, the driver was prepared to become involved in a shoot-out.

'Take the boy inside,' Nylund told the driver, who was noticeably relieved that Nylund didn't need him alongside. 'I'll go see what's happening.'

'Let me show you,' the boy offered.

Nylund refused him. 'Go back inside, lad.'

Colt drawn, Nylund led the way to the front of the building. Once the boy and stage driver were safely inside, he went off to investigate the disturbance in the prairie. From that distance he was unable to make out the various outlines that flitted in front of him. Trying to keep his body low to the ground, he ran with his back bent, glad that his sand-covered clothes allowed him to blend with the scenery. Closer and closer he got, the blurred shapes becoming clearer.

Slipping the Colt back into its holster, Nylund knew he wouldn't be needing it for his own defence. The attackers who were in front of him didn't have Nylund as their chosen victim.

Lying flat on the ground was the driver who had gone off in search of the horses. Vultures swooped on the corpse, flapping their wings as they soared back into the sky. Whipping off his hat, Nylund swung his arms wildly, trying to frighten them away. He was reluctant to use the Colt, knowing that the sound of gunfire would only serve to alarm the occupants of the shack. Unnerved by Nylund's arrival, the birds retreated, but only a short distance.

Kneeling down by the body Nylund turned the man over onto his back, his stomach churning at the sight of the bloody mess of the driver's face. In the sandy ground were the hoof prints of horses. It was difficult to tell how many there may have been, perhaps just one, as the prints were on top of each other, blurring the impressions in the dust. The injury to the man's face was synonymous with being kicked by a horse, his nose having been smashed by the force. It was ironic that the man had been successful in finding the horses, only to be killed by one. Nylund knew he couldn't leave him he was, for he deserved to be buried, his body protected from becoming prey.

Covering the body as best he could with his own coat, Nylund knew it afforded little protection from the sharp claws and beaks of the awaiting vultures. Running back to the shack, Nylund slowed to a walk as he neared it, trying not to show any outward panic or distress.

'What was it?' The driver came out to meet Nylund, the shotgun in his hands, his knuckles white. He wasn't a man who took easily to the role as he was now playing, and it was something of a strain for him.

Nylund broke the news gently to him, having no idea how long the men had worked together. Even though Nylund did his best to soften the blow it still came as a shock to the driver, his face going pale.

'I'll try to find a shovel, or something that will act as one,' Nylund explained. 'Then I can bury him.'

'Wait a moment, and I'll come with you.'

'No, you'll be best here.' Nylund was thinking of the man's feelings; seeing a friend battered as his was would only upset and disturb him. 'I'll ask the preacher to come, that way he can do his job, too.'

The driver didn't push the idea, sensing Nylund was trying to find excuses for him not to come.

Tut-tutting as he viewed the lifeless body the preacher mumbled a few well-chosen words, before settling down to watch as Nylund dug a shallow grave.

Though the earth was gritty it was tightly packed, and Nylund had to work hard to break through. The heavy shovel he had found at the rear of the shack helped him in his task, though not making the work easy.

'How old would you think he was?' asked the preacher, Bible clutched in his hands as he waited to perform his final duties.

'I wouldn't think he had reached his middle twenties,' mused Nylund, taking a break from digging. Having already thrown off his shirt he was still unbearably hot.

'There's too much dying,' said the preacher mournfully.

'Death is a fact of life,' replied Nylund, knowing that someone more intelligent and better educated would say something more original.

Not wanting to get involved in any further conversation, Nylund carried on digging, his work preventing the preacher from speaking.

With the hole dug to the depth of his knees, Nylund lowered the man's body into the grave, quickly covering it with earth, the preacher praying over the grave as he did so.

'I'm finished here,' the preacher announced, as he bestowed a final blessing. 'I'll walk back to the building.'

'All right,' Nylund nodded. The elderly man looked tired. Already worn out by the events of the last two days, this second burial had strained him even further. Nylund watched as the preacher walked away, dragging his tired legs along the sandy floor.

Finally covering the body, Nylund stacked rocks at the head of the grave, forming a makeshift cross. Collecting his hat, shirt and coat Nylund followed the preacher back toward the shack. Going round to the rear he removed his gunbelt, threw it down on top of his clothes, then drew a bucket of water from the well. Scooping water from the bucket he splashed it over his face, washing off the sweat and sand that had stuck to his skin. Tipping up the bucket he poured the remainder over his body, letting it chase away some of the tiredness and enliven his muscles.

He dropped the bucket down the well again and drew it back up. Catching hold of the base of the bucket Nylund tipped the cool water over his head. Eyes closed he placed the bucket back on the wall, rubbing the heels of his palms over his eyelids.

There was a loud crack, and the earth was ploughed up between Nylund's feet. Leaping back, his reflexes were so quick it was difficult for him to judge how close he had been to being injured by what was definitely a rifle shot. Looking up from the groove that had suddenly appeared in the ground, he saw, standing no more than ten feet from him, a man holding a rifle that was aimed his way.

The man facing Nylund must have been in his seventies. Though his body could have passed for that of a man thirty years his junior, his face was old and lined. A crooked smile on his lips revealed few teeth remaining, and these were black. A large hat covered his head, underneath which a mop of white hair stuck out at all angles. None of this perturbed Nylund as much as the man's next action, for he threw his head back, the hat falling off, and with an ear-piercing shriek, cried:

'Yee haw! Yee haw!'

Nylund was staggered. He briefly forgot his concentration on the rifle to stare in disbelief at the man.

'Yee haw! Yee haw!'

Moving slowly to the left, Nylund could feel his holster against his ankle. Considering it too much of a risk to make a dive for the Colt while the rifle was on him, Nylund gave up on the idea.

From the corner of his eye he caught movement; it was the stage driver, shotgun in his hands, slowly moving around to the rear of the building. His back close to the wall, the man was being cautious. Weighing up the situation before deciding on what action to take, he hadn't just run out into the thick of it, risking both his and Nylund's well-being.

With a slight movement of his fingers, Nylund waved the stage driver back, wanting him to retain some cover for as long as he could.

'Yee haw! Yee haw!'

The old man continued to yelp, his cries becoming louder. The rifle shaking in his hands before he lowered it to his side, Nylund seized his chance. Diving for his holster, he held it still with one hand, drawing the Colt with the other. Rolling his body across the ground to make himself more of a difficult target, Nylund had the man in his sights. Revolver cocked, he was ready to fire.

'Drop the rifle!' Nylund shouted. He wasn't going to shoot unless it became absolutely necessary. At present the man posed no threat. The earlier danger had passed.

'Yee haw! Yee haw!'

It was obvious Nylund hadn't got through to the man, so he shouted once more.

'Put the rifle down.'

The stock of the rifle fell from the man's hand, hitting the ground with a thud. He kept hold of the barrel with the fingers of his other hand, so that now the rifle was upright.

Relieved that he had at least achieved part of his intention, Nylund spoke again, this time his voice not so demanding.

'Let go of the rifle.'

Nylund's palms were sweating so much that the butt was becoming slippery in his grip. Were he to have cause to fire Nylund doubted whether he would be able to.

Getting to his feet, his mouth almost

falling open in amazement, Nylund watched as the man, resting one finger on the end of the barrel, circled it in some crazy dance.

NINE

Taking the rifle from the man, Nylund viewed him with some bewilderment. He was thinking both of his own safety and that of the man's. The old man's actions didn't promote confidence in his mental stability.

As Nylund took away the prop of the rifle the man collapsed onto the ground, his fall almost graceful. He had not collapsed heavily, nor, it seemed, had he injured himself in any way. There he sat, looking up at Nylund, a huge grin across his grey face.

Coming closer to get a better look, the stage driver turned Nylund's way, shaking his head and shrugging his shoulders.

'Who is he?' asked the driver, his question earning him a smile from the man sitting on the ground.

'I should imagine he's the person responsible for moving my bedroll, and hiding my bag,' decided Nylund, pleased now that the mystery had been solved.

'And where did he come from?'

It was Nylund's turn to shrug his shoulders. 'Your guess is as good as mine. I don't think we've much chance of getting a sensible answer from him.'

Telling the man to get up, Nylund was surprised when he rose to his feet, obeying the order.

'I'll check him for guns,' Nylund told the driver. He nodded toward the weapon the driver still held in his hands. 'You keep an eye on him.'

The old man had several layers of clothing on, despite the extreme heat, and Nylund was occupied for some time checking in the pockets of each garment, his search fruitless.

'What's happening out here?' The preacher tottered from the shack. 'We heard the gunshot, then nothing further, is everyone all right?'

'Everything is fine, preacher,' Nylund told him. 'Now if you'd go back inside.'

The stage driver shepherded the man of the cloth back inside, assuring him that Nylund had everything under control.

'He might be a crazy old fool,' Nylund told the driver when he returned. 'But at least he tells us one thing – that it's possible to survive out here.'

'You call what he is surviving?' questioned the driver.

'I see a body and soul joined together,' remarked Nylund. 'So, maybe his mind is crazy, but that doesn't change the fact he's alive.'

'I'm mighty pleased to meet you.' The old man took Nylund's hand, pumping it in greeting. 'The name's Franklin Ford.'

'Matt Nylund.' Taken aback by the man's sudden comprehension of the situation, Nylund told him his name.

As Nylund was wondering whether Franklin Ford's instability was nothing more than a pretence the man proved him wrong by launching into another round of laughter.

'Yee haw! It's mighty nice to meet you. Yee haw!'

Maybe all wasn't lost, Nylund reasoned. Perhaps in the few rational moments Franklin Ford had he could learn more of him, and discover a way he could bring help to the passengers.

'Why don't you take him inside,' Nylund suggested to the driver. 'Maybe getting out of this heat will help him.'

Taking the old man by the arm, the driver led him round to the front door of the shack, Nylund hearing a final 'Yee haw!' before they went inside.

Being totally ignorant of who the man was and where he came from, Nylund was determined to find out more. It was obvious that the man was connected with the shack, yet he couldn't be living in it, for the place was thick with dust that hadn't been disturbed for a very long time. The building was very small and Nylund had investigated most of it, with the exception of the lean-to at the rear.

The lean-to wasn't very big, and as Nylund pulled open the door to look inside he could see it was even smaller than he had first believed. Unlike the interior of the shack the lean-to wasn't dusty, nor was the air stale, as gaps in the woodwork allowed the breeze to circulate in the small space.

The light that filled the lean-to allowed Nylund to study its interior, and it wasn't what he had expected. Assuming, even before opening the door, that this lean-to was where Franklin Ford lived, Nylund, instead of finding a jumble of possessions, had discovered a well laid out store of mainly food; enough provisions to feed the group of passengers for several days. Picking up a potato, Nylund squeezed it in his hand, finding the vegetable to be firm and edible, the coolness of the small lean-to having kept it fresh. Not used to organizing meals for more than one person, he left the food where it was. Deciding to appoint either the preacher's or the attorney's wife to take care of the cooking and preparing of the food, Nylund firmly shut the door of the lean-to before returning to the shack.

Stepping into the shady building he allowed his eyes a few seconds to adjust to the change from bright sunlight to semi-darkness. There was a movement of shadowy figures, and, when finally accustomed to the dimness, Nylund was able to identify them.

Franklin Ford, his foot tapping in time with a tune that only he could hear, was trying to get the preacher's wife to dance. The stage driver, while holding his rifle in one hand, was trying to separate Ford from the woman, and failing. Walking across the shack, Nylund seized Ford by the tops of his arms. Squeezing hard, he forced him to release the grip he had on the preacher's wife's hands. Then, partly lifting the man off the floor, he pulled him across the shack. Opening the door he threw him out into the desert. Following, Nylund stood over the man.

'I don't know what you're doing here. And

maybe you have more rights to this place than we have,' Nylund began, pointing a finger at the man. 'But while we are here you are going to behave yourself. Your idea of a welcome with gunfire wasn't what I'd call friendly.'

'Listen up a minute.' The driver came out of the building behind Nylund and called him over, wanting a private word. 'Careful what you're doing, this ain't no old fool you've got there.'

'What?'

'He's some kind of trader. I think it might be guns to the Indians. From what I got from him it seems he's out here for a purpose. Every couple of weeks or so some men come along, supply him with food and whatever he needs. In return he gives them the gold he's got from the Indians in exchange for the guns. I gather that these mystery men steal the weapons then get him to act as a go-between.'

Nylund laughed in disbelief.

'You believe that? And when did he tell

you all this? In between the "Yees" and the "haas"?'

'I know it sounds ridiculous, but he didn't say it so clearly, I read between the lines and picked it out.'

'Why would anyone, even taking into regard that they're criminals, have anything to do with an old crazy like him?'

'I think you've said it yourself. Because he is crazy; he doesn't need to be trusted. If he gets caught in his illegal trade no one is going to take any notice of what he says.'

Nylund thought for a moment. It did seem plausible. The driver was right in all he said, and, for the time being, Nylund was prepared to accept it.

'Have you any inkling who these men could be?'

'No, but I'd figure it to be an awful big coincidence if there were two gangs working in these parts.'

'They're the same ones who ambushed the stage?' Nylund realized the driver was thinking ahead of him.

'It stands to reason.'

Nodding his head, Nylund knew he couldn't get away from the evidence that faced him.

'When was the last time these men came?'

'I don't know,' the driver admitted, offering, 'though I can find out from him, I'm sure.'

'No, I don't think there's any need,' Nylund told him. 'There's a store of food out the back that would last one man several weeks. That gives us food. Unfortunately we have no way of getting out of here. I thought he might have a horse or mule.'

'So did I, but if he did then he would be able to get away from here. While he's trapped here he has no choice but to go along with these men.'

'And how does he get these weapons to the Indians?' Nylund asked.

'I don't know, that I haven't worked out yet.'

'Whatever,' Nylund lightened the seriousness of their conversation. 'Let's take one thing at a time. We've got shade, water and food. Not so long ago I doubted we'd ever find that.'

'Would either of you men have a bottle of whisky on you?' The old man became lucid again, even if his request was unexpected.

Nylund shook his head, then answered: 'No, sorry.'

The two women had come out to prepare a stew for the group over a fire Nylund had built outside the shack. Even though it was hot food on a hot day, when it was ready it was very welcome and satisfied everyone's hunger.

'That's mighty fine cooking, ladies,' Nylund complimented the preacher and attorney's wives after he had finished the meal.

'Will you be leaving us?' The attorney's wife spoke to Nylund, reluctance in her voice at starting a conversation.

'Of course he will be,' snapped her husband, the first time he had spoken in a long time. 'We can't just stay here, can we?'

'No, I don't suppose so,' the wife whispered. Her head down, she avoided looking at any of the others.

It was only now that Nylund finally had the attorney figured. He was a bully, yet, like all bullies, he was a coward underneath. Threatening women and frightening the weak passengers took little strength of character; he had even tried to bully Nylund, while standing behind a gun.

Once everyone had finished eating, Nylund went to the well and drew a bucket of water for the women to wash the pots and pans that they had used in feeding the group.

'Will you be leaving us?' The attorney's wife had followed Nylund to the well, standing alongside him as he pulled up the bucket.

'Yes.' He answered without turning her way.

'When?'

'I'll take a few hours' sleep, then when it gets dark I'll leave.'

Nylund could sense the woman wanted to say more, yet there was a reticence to her that he couldn't fathom.

'I will find help, and I'll be back with it,' he assured her, wondering if it was fear they would not be rescued that had her remain silent. 'And you'll be safe here. There's food and water.'

'I know that, it's just that ... I don't really want to say this, but I feel I must warn you.'

'Warn me of what?' Disturbed by what she said Nylund wanted to know more. 'What is it?'

'It's my husband, he can become impatient.'

'Impatient?' Nylund exclaimed disgustedly, then remembered his manners. 'I don't mean to be unkind, but your husband suffers from a little more than impatience.'

'He had a wonderful future ahead of him, and it lies west, where we were heading,' the woman continued, finding it easier now to talk to Nylund, 'which is why he became heated earlier. We need to get to our destination quickly, and I fear that if we have to stay here for any length of time he could explode again.'

‘I won’t let you stay here for a minute longer than I have to,’ Nylund told her. ‘And I’d by far prefer to be waiting here than have to make the journey I’m going to.’

‘I’ll try to explain that to him,’ she went on. ‘But he can be difficult.’

‘Would you like me to...’ Nylund didn’t have the chance to finish his offer before she interjected.

‘No, no, no! Don’t do that. That would only make him worse.’ She smiled up at Nylund. ‘I’ll speak to him. I’ll do my best.’

Watching her walk away, Nylund felt nothing but pity for her; not long married and already the attorney was ruining her life. Maybe the man had another side to him, one that she loved, but Nylund found it near impossible to think of him in any other way. The man was just a selfish bully.

Even if the wife could talk sense into the attorney, Nylund thought it cautionary to speak to the stage driver, warning him that he could experience problems with the man. Yet what disturbance he could cause other than a slight one, Nylund couldn't think. There was no chance of him leading the other passengers away from the security of the shack, with its food and water, out into a hostile prairie. They had trusted Nylund this far, they wouldn't lose faith in him now.

'If he wants to wander off,' Nylund told the driver, 'I suggest you don't try to stop him, just take care of the others.'

'What about him?' The stage driver nodded at the crazy Franklin Ford, who was propped against the wall of the shack, his arm going rapidly up and down as he played an imaginary fiddle.

'Just keep him away from the food, and...' Nylund added as an afterthought, 'the women.'

Recalling the old fool's earlier attempt at getting the preacher's wife to dance he thought it better not to risk any further upsets.

'Why don't you take charge as from now? I need some sleep before I leave.'

Nylund left the man and wandered off to

the rear of the building where he could rest without disturbance. The others were still euphoric at having reached safety, and were talking around the fire. Their chatter would keep Nylund awake.

With both body and mind tired, Nylund still found it difficult to sleep. Though not a man accustomed to failure, he had a niggling fear at the back of his mind that he might not be successful in finding help; the prairie was vast, it would be easy to become lost. He admitted to himself that it had only been by chance that he had stumbled across the cabin. He could just as easily have passed it by. Nylund sweated, his clothes sticking uncomfortably to his body; it wasn't heat that had him sweating, it was a cold fear, so many lives depended on his decisions. He knew that by taking them away from the route of the stage line he was risking them never being discovered, yet if he had let them stay there, all that would be found would be corpses.

Finally Nylund found peace and was able

to sleep, and would have done so for many hours if coldness hadn't woken him. With darkness falling he decided that now would be the best time to leave. In the shack he collected his bag and bedroll. The passengers still sat outside the building, the stage driver holding them enthralled with stories of what, to Nylund, seemed such an adventurous past that he would have to be over two hundred years old to have fitted it all in. Still, it entertained the people, and that at present was what was important.

There was no need to make a fuss and announce his departure, so Nylund slipped away quietly. Once they found his bag and bedroll missing they would know he had gone. As Nylund walked off he could hear the voices of the passengers; their laughter carried to his ears and he had to force himself onwards, wanting to return to the shack and its relative comfort. But they were relying on him, so, head down, Nylund carried on, and soon walked out of hearing range.

Alone once more, Nylund felt better. He

wasn't a sociable man, and preferred solitude to company. With a plan to return to the stage line route and follow it, Nylund knew that as long as the food and water he carried with him lasted he was in with a chance of finding help. Though it had to be natural to think of his own welfare, Nylund feared that if something happened to him, the others ran the risk of never being found. For this reason he felt he had to make sure of his own safety.

Planning to make his way back to where the stage had been burnt out, Nylund intended to spend the hottest part of the day there, resting in the shadow of a large rock cluster. He would then decide whether he would follow the tracks of the stage backwards, or make his own way forward. Even though the urgency had gone from the situation, Nylund still found himself hurrying and had to consciously slow his pace, otherwise he would tire himself early. He was also worried about the possibility of the men who supplied Franklin Ford with weapons for the Indians returning to the shack before either he or help reached it. If, as he and the stage driver strongly suspected, they were also the men who had ambushed the stage, Nylund prayed that he returned first.

The men had already committed a crime that would lead them to the gallows if they were caught; discovering the victims of their crime at their own hide-out might force them to commit a more heinous act. It was this thought that made Nylund want to go back and give the passengers his protection, but who then would go out and try to find help? Definitely not the attorney. With his selfishness he would be unreliable; the preacher was too old; the boy too young; and the stage driver, Nylund felt, wouldn't have the confidence to go alone. That left only him.

There was nothing he could do with these worries other than push them from his mind and carry on with his journey. Fortunately, Nylund was a healthy man and the exercise he had taken over the last couple of days hadn't taken too much of a toll on his body. The muscles in his legs were becoming painful though and when he stopped to rest they became stiff, making it more difficult when he moved on.

When dawn arrived Nylund found himself still walking. Knowing that he didn't have much further to go he paused to take a sip of water, then trudged on. All the time he was wondering what was happening back at the shack. How would they be spending today, tomorrow, and all the days that passed until he returned? Whatever they were doing they were doing it at least twelve hours walk away from him. Nylund couldn't change a thing, so there was no point in him worrying.

When he finally reached the burnt-out stage Nylund was just about ready to collapse, and with some relief he found a shady spot and settled down to rest until nightfall returned.

TEN

Nylund took a short sleep. When he awoke, refreshed and ready to go, he had to force himself to stay put in the shade. It wasn't his style to lie around and while the time away uselessly, but it was all Nylund could do. To get up and walk on would be a mistake. In a very short time he would become exhausted and thirsty. Both energy and water were things he had to conserve.

The time until nightfall would have to be passed in some way that would prevent Nylund from becoming bored; his thoughts wandered from the past, through the present, and into the future. He considered what he would have liked to change, where he would now prefer to be, and what his future held. The answers came more or less simply to him; as for the past he would change everything he could, it was only unavoidable situations and circumstances that had created the man he now was. When thinking of the present, he would rather be anywhere than here; and of the future, he didn't really care what it held for him. Of course, he hoped it would be better than the past. There was very little more he could ask for.

Stripping off his coat and shirt, Nylund tried to get his body accustomed to the heat. Even though he was out of direct sunlight it was still unbearably hot. If the temperature remained constant through day and night he could possibly get used to it, since there would be no alternative; but, where the nights became bitterly cold, and the heavy coat he wore wasn't enough to keep the chill from his body, he would never be able to adapt himself.

When thinking of his own condition was no longer enough to fully occupy his mind, Nylund tried to decide whether or not to retrace the tracks of the stage, which would be a lot easier than going on and finding his own way.

He chose to go back, if only because he knew for certain that help lay there. Even though help could also be just a day or so's walk away in the other direction, he couldn't take that chance. Finding that he was taking an occasional sip of water to break the monotony of the day, he determined to drink only when thirsty, otherwise his supply would be gone in no time at all.

Pulling off his boots, Nylund massaged the toes and soles of his swollen feet, then quickly put the boots back on before the swelling of his feet prevented him from doing so.

To Nylund's surprise he fell asleep again, the sun's heat having made him dozy. It was dark when he awoke. Quickly putting his shirt and coat on, Nylund made himself ready for the journey. Eager to be going, he scrambled to his feet; ahead of him the moonlight made the tracks of the stage easy to see, and Nylund began his walk, every step taking him further from the shack and the stage passengers.

From the corner of an eye, he caught a glimpse of something moving. Looking left he saw a glow in the sky. So distant was the source of the illumination that it cast only a dim glow. Nylund was keen to discover more; there was no point in him following the stagecoach's track when help could lie much nearer. With investigation in mind, Nylund turned off his path and, with the glow in the sky as his guide, walked toward it.

It took some time for him to realize that he was indeed getting closer, for the glow in the sky only gradually grew a shade brighter. Nylund didn't know what was causing it, but as he walked on his suspicions began to grow. The light could be caused by a camp fire, and probably a large camp-fire, one that possibly cooked food for, and warmed, eight men. It was too much of a coincidence for Nylund to think anything other than it was the stage ambushers. This seemed to be the area in which they had been staying for some time. Obviously the bandits were camped at a waterhole of which Nylund had no knowledge. Along with the ambush they were no doubt also responsible for the weapon trade with the Indians.

As Nylund got closer he found his suspicions confirmed. A large camp fire burned, the warm air that rose from it carrying across the desert. In the darkness Nylund had little need for cover. He would be difficult to see, but the silence made it necessary for him to go quietly. The slightest noise could give him away, and the consequences of that were obvious to him.

Nearer now, he could see the bodies of eight sleeping men lying close to the fire, snores and other nocturnal noises coming to his ears. They hadn't posted a guard, apparently not believing they needed one. For this Nylund was thankful. Why he was here, or what he intended to do, Nylund didn't know.

To discover it was definitely the ambushers had come as such a shock that his thoughts were momentarily lost. He could shoot them where they lay – but that was cowardly, his own morals and principles wouldn't allow that. Even to shoot a fully conscious man in the back was abhorrent to him. But, having regard to his own personal safety, if he wanted to capture them, or hand out his own punishment, that was the only option open to him. It wouldn't be possible to disarm them all. After a first warning shot from him he would be riddled with lead. The time had now come when he had to face the truth, that all he could do was merely observe, then slip away and continue on his walk in search of help.

A movement and a horse's whinny caught Nylund's attention. Scrambling across the ground, trying to stay low, being so close to the men now as to be easily spotted, Nylund got across to the horses. Raising himself up slowly to his full height so as not to alarm the remuda, Nylund had a plan formulating. In a kind of rough justice he could turn the tables on the men and leave them stranded.

All it would take was for him to cut the ropes of the temporary corral, and the animals would be loose. Nylund's mind seized on this idea. Drawing his knife he slashed the ropes nearest to him. Discovering themselves free, the first horses began to move away. He cautiously moved the other horses close to where he had cut the rope. He would drive them off in one go, but first the sight of a stationary wagon caught his interest so much that he felt he should investigate the contents of its sheeted-down back. Dropping to the ground, he propelled himself along with his elbows, trying to stay as low as possible. Grabbing hold of the spokes of a wheel Nylund pulled himself upright. The sheet across the wagon was so tight that he had to cut the side ropes. Nylund peered in. Long narrow crates filled the back, packed in so tightly it wasn't possible to get the blade of a knife between them. Levering open the crate nearest to him, the wooden top splintering loudly, Nylund froze. He was sure the noise would have disturbed one of the men. Close by there was a faint mumbling which soon died. After a couple of minutes, Nylund allowed himself to move again. Gently he pulled at the crate's top, pushing his fingers into the gap he had created. Beneath his fingers was a coldness; a coldness that could only be metal. Running his fingers left to right, Nylund was able to create a mental picture of rifles. The single crate had to hold at least twenty weapons. There had to be fifty or more crates in total in the wagon; Nylund wasn't a man who was good with numbers, but he knew it added up to an awful lot of firearms. Closing the lid, trying to make good the damage he had caused, Nylund left the wagon, returning to the horses as quickly, yet also as quietly, as possible.

The rifles were no doubt heading for the Indians, which meant that perhaps on the day fast-approaching the men would be delivering them to the shack. It was a priority for Nylund to either stop or delay them from doing so. The urgency had changed from finding help to saving the passengers from further harm.

Moving back along the row of horses Nylund began to herd them. With hooves smashing into the ground beside him Nylund felt uneasy close to the big, powerful animals. It would take only one kick to kill a man, as the assistant stage driver had been kicked to death. The horses brushed against Nylund's shoulders, his presence disturbing them. Stamping their hooves, the horses began to whinny and neigh. Nylund hurried, for the animals would soon be attracting attention with their behaviour.

'What's going on there?' a man's voice barked out through the darkness.

For a second Nylund stayed perfectly still, hoping that the horses' behaviour would be disregarded. But it wasn't. The voice called out again.

'What's happening?' The voice, this time, was clearer and more urgent, the caller obviously now free of drowsiness.

If Nylund didn't make some move soon he

knew the man would be coming over to investigate. It was time for Nylund to try a deception and call the man's bluff.

'Nothin'. Go back to sleep.'

For a second Nylund believed it had worked, only for his hopes to be shattered when the man shouted again.

'Is that you, Munroe?'

Nylund didn't know whether to answer yes or no. The question could be a trick, or it could be genuine. Whatever it was, Nylund had to take a risk.

'Yeah, it's me, Munroe.'

The gunshot came as a surprise, yet it wasn't aimed at Nylund, who, standing amid the horses, would be difficult to hit, but was fired into the night sky to raise the alarm.

Nylund knew he had been discovered, and had to make his escape. There was no time now for him to drive off all the horses as he had planned. All he could do was hope to get away. A strong and good rider, Nylund leapt up onto the back of a nearby horse. Wrapping his fingers tightly into the animal's mane, he kicked its flanks, sending the horse shooting off. Leaping what was left of the rope corral as if it wasn't there, Nylund was only just able to cling on. As shots whistled past him, he considered returning the fire, but thought it unwise, needing all his wits to stay on his mount.

Nylund at present had no control over where he was heading, and he didn't bother with any attempt to check the horse, which would only have risked slowing it. Even the joy of travelling under a power other than his own couldn't take the seriousness of the situation from the fore of Nylund's mind. After riding at speed for some time, Nylund forcibly slowed the horse, and after a brief battle of wits the horse reduced his pace.

Man and horse had travelled far, but also in an arc, which meant that though they had put a great deal of distance between them and the ambushers, they were now much closer to the shack. Instinct told Nylund he should go back to the shack, common sense telling him that very soon that was where trouble would be erupting. On the other hand he could see the wisdom of riding away from it all, thereby saving his own skin. He could also see the utter selfishness. It wasn't a difficult decision for Nylund to make. He chose to go back.

Riding the horse was now difficult for Nylund, for he had little control over it. Remaining on the horse's back, not wanting to give it the chance to run off, and leave him stranded once again, he created reins of a fashion from the straps of his water-bottles. It wasn't an ideal arrangement, but fortunately the horse didn't object too much, and soon become used to the idea.

Nylund's movements were almost as one with those of the horse beneath him and they covered the same ground with ease, that Nylund, not so long ago, had laboured over.

Nylund was confident that the men had not been able to get a clear view of him, but it wouldn't take even the dumbest long to work out who he was. There could be no other person walking across the desert in the middle of the night.

At another time, in different circumstances, Nylund would have taken time out to cover his tracks. There was no point now in wasting his time doing that, it didn't matter if they followed him, for ultimately they had the same destination. The horse was fresh and in good health. He wouldn't need to stop to recover from his exertions until they reached the shack. Stealing the horse had raised Nylund's spirits. Though he was aware the worst was yet to come, he also knew that had he not spotted the glow in the sky from the camp-fire he would have carried on his walk in total ignorance of the perils soon to face the passengers. By going back he was doing something for them. What he could achieve Nylund didn't know, but he wouldn't be leaving them, with all respect for the stage driver's ability, close to defenceless.

Whether he would have the time to move the passengers from the shack and find them a new sanctuary, Nylund didn't know. It wasn't the most plausible of ideas. Even if he could do it, there was the problem of that fool Franklin Ford to overcome. He would be sure to tell the men of the passengers having stayed there and there was no chance that they would disregard this as just one of the old man's crazy fantasies, for it was too close to the truth. Which meant Nylund would have to take Ford with them, and with Ford missing the ambushers would become worried, he being their vital link with the Indians. They couldn't afford to lose him, and doubtlessly they would come looking ... their search probably leading to Nylund and the people he would be protecting.

With the lives of the others at risk, Nylund felt he couldn't really make decisions for them. He had, of course, had to make decisions for them before but that was when the only options open to them were to follow him to shelter, or stay in the hot desert and certainly die. Yet now they still only had two options, neither better than the other, either to stay and undoubtedly fight, or flee and be tracked like animals. The ambushers could no longer let them go free, for the passengers knew too much about their illegal operations.

Nylund would inform them of their choices, then respect the decision they made, whether it was unanimous or not. The false dawn was rising, and before long, if not already, the ambushers would be on his trail. In their position Nylund would have waited for the light of dawn before setting off. The men had nothing to lose by delaying their chase. Though he couldn't be sure what head start he had on them, Nylund was sure it could be counted in hours. Rounding up the few horses that he had managed to set free would occupy them for some time.

The shack was not too far off and Nylund knew that if he continued riding at the same pace he had averaged over the journey he would be there within the next hour. As the morning sun rose, Nylund saw the ridge that marked the location of the shack ahead of him. The sight was a very welcome one.

Head down close to the horse's neck, Nylund dug in his knees, and clinging on he raced toward the shack that had now come into view. A bright oil-lamp that was being drowned out by the brilliant early-morning light stood in the empty window-frame. As he rode closer, Nylund saw the lamp being extinguished. The barrel of a rifle appeared in the corner of the frame, aimed in Nylund's direction. He slowed the horse and sat upright as far as he could without feeling too insecure from the lack of a saddle. The last thing he wanted now was to be shot.

'It's me!' Nylund shouted. Taking off his stetson he waved it in the air above his head. 'I'm back.'

The weapon was drawn back from the window and the door of the shack opened wide, the stage driver stepping out into the morning air, holding the rifle in the crook of his arm.

'You've found help?' the man asked, trying

hard to contain his mounting excitement.

Slipping down from the horse's back, Nylund shook his head, seeing the man's face fall, disappointment now clearly evident on it.

'Can you get me a rope?' Nylund asked, needing to secure the horse.

Leaving the rifle in Nylund's custody, the stage driver disappeared round the rear of the building, returning and handing over a thick, heavy rope, which Nylund used to tie up the horse.

'Let's go inside,' Nylund suggested. He didn't want to have to repeat what he had to say, and it would be best that they all heard it together.

The five passengers were in varying states of consciousness; the attorney and his wife were awake, the youngster, bleary-eyed, had only just awoken when Nylund entered the building and the preacher and his wife were both asleep.

'I have something to tell you,' Nylund began, his voice waking the preacher, who turned to shake his wife into consciousness.

'Wake up, wake up, dear. He's back, we're safe.'

'No,' Nylund raised a hand to stop him. Safe was the last thing they were, but he didn't want to announce it in an alarmist way. It would be best to break the news to them gently. It wasn't going to be easy, but he had to make it quick. Time was vital, they needed to take advantage of every minute they could.

'Then why are you back?' the preacher asked accusingly, as if Nylund was at fault.

'I have something to tell you,' Nylund repeated, then told them all that had happened over the last few hours, ending with the two options. 'So, we can leave here now, or stay.'

'Where can we go?' the preacher asked.

Nylund shrugged his shoulders. It was the only answer he could give.

'And if we stay?' It was the attorney's wife who asked Nylund the question.

'We have to fight. They won't be coming

here to make friends with us.' Nylund saw no point in hiding the truth. 'Leaving us alive would be too much of a risk for them to take. Their criminal activities are far more important to them than our lives.'

'If we go, will they come after us?' the preacher's wife wanted to know.

'Undoubtedly,' Nylund nodded, 'and with us on foot, and them on horseback, it won't take them long to catch up.'

The passengers looked at each other, each hoping that someone would come up with the glimmer of an idea.

'Let's have a show of hands,' Nylund suggested. 'First, who wants to stay?' He counted the raised hands.

ELEVEN

'And who wants to go?' He counted the raised hands, grabbing the arm of Franklin Ford, pulling it down. 'You have no vote.'

With Ford's hand now down, it left only one hand raised, that of the attorney.

'So it looks like we stay,' Nylund said. 'Five to one carries it.'

'And what is your choice?' the preacher asked Nylund.

'I'm not exercising my vote,' replied Nylund with a smile. 'I prefer to stay impartial.'

'What happens now?' asked the stage driver.

'We prepare ourselves for visitors.' Nylund's answer sounded simple, but was far from it. He turned to the boy. 'Can you take the horse around the back, and get it out of sight as best you can? There's no point in advertising our presence.'

The youngster nodded, then went out.

'Hey, get down off there!' Nylund shouted. Looking out of the door he had seen the boy climb up onto the back of the animal.

'I'm not doing any harm,' argued the youngster.

'He can do you far more harm than you can him,' maintained Nylund. He didn't want to have brought the boy this far only to have him fall from the horse and break bones.

'He won't hurt me.' The boy leant forward to stroke the horse's neck, speaking to him softly. 'Will you?'

It was the first time Nylund had seen the boy so confident, he had come alive on the back of the animal.

Backing the horse up, the boy prepared to ride it round to the rear of the shack, handling the animal like an expert.

'How come you're such a good rider?' Nylund asked, no longer angry with the boy.

'My pa taught me. I was riding before I

could walk.'

'How far do you reckon you could ride at speed?' Nylund had the beginning of an idea.

'You're not thinking of sending the boy for help, are you?' the preacher asked Nylund, the tone in his voice clearly showing he disapproved of the idea.

'Well?' Nylund waited for the boy to answer, deliberately ignoring the preacher.

'I could ride as far as any horse can carry me,' stated the boy proudly.

'Have you got a saddle around here?' Nylund asked Ford, getting nothing more than a blank look in return.

'There's one out back, in the lean-to.' The stage driver came to Nylund. 'I saw it earlier.'

'Then take him round back and fix the horse up.' Nylund issued the order to the driver, and was quickly obeyed.

'You can't send that young child for help,' the preacher insisted.

'Then would you rather he stayed here to risk getting killed with the rest of us?' Nylund's reply was chilling, and he could see it distressed the preacher. 'This way the boy gets a chance to save himself.'

'I'm sorry,' the religious man apologized meekly. 'I hadn't thought of it in that way.'

At the rear of the building Nylund found the stage driver helping the boy saddle up the horse. They had found a bridle and reins too. Retrieving the straps of his water-bottles, which he had used as makeshift reins, Nylund secured them to the bottles once again, refilling them from the well. From the lean-to he took food, packing it into the pockets of the boy's coat. The youngster would be leaving far better prepared than Nylund had.

Swinging himself up onto the back of the animal, the youngster regained his confidence, becoming a different person to the shy boy that had travelled in the stage. Nylund handed him the water-bottles, together with a word of caution.

'If the horse gets tired, rest him, if he gets thirsty then give him a drink,' he advised.

'And the same goes for you, take care of yourself.' Noticing the youngster's head was bare Nylund took off his own stetson, and gave it to the boy. 'That'll keep the sun off you.'

'Thank you.'

'Good luck, lad,' Nylund wished him well, 'head toward the sunrise and you won't go wrong.'

Nylund was sure that help lay in that direction. It was roughly along that path that the stagecoach had been travelling. After walking round to the front of the shack behind the horse Nylund and the stage driver watched as the boy rode off, leaving a clear set of tracks behind him. The boy's going served many purposes, including the fact that the horse-tracks leading from the shack would probably convince the ambushers that the man who had stolen their horse was no longer there. That gave the passengers a slight advantage, one that Nylund wanted to exploit to its fullest.

'Shall we go back inside?' Nylund suggested to the stage driver. Circumstances had now made them equal, and Nylund didn't feel comfortable issuing orders. Though the driver was ready to be led by Nylund, he could also sense the change in their relationship.

Back inside the shack, Nylund made a survey of their weapons. There was his own Colt, the stage driver's rifle, and the rifle they had taken from the crazy Franklin Ford. It wasn't much of an arsenal, yet it would have to do. The Colt staying in his holster, Nylund took the derringer back from the driver, and handed it over to the attorney.

'If you have cause to, make good use of that.'

'I will,' the lawyer agreed, pleased to have the weapon returned. While he and Nylund had a mutual enemy their own differences were briefly forgotten.

Grabbing the large table Nylund turned it over onto its side, the table-top now able to act as a shield.

'I'd prefer you ladies to sit behind here,' he

told the two women. 'And you too, preacher. It's better you have some protection if, and I pray it's if, the lead starts to fly.'

'You think they may resort to violence?' asked thc preacher nervously.

'I don't see them sitting down at a tea-party to discuss it with us,' replied Nylund sharply, trying to impress on the preacher the type of men these were.

'They're on their way, I can see riders!' the stage driver, standing at the window-frame, called to Nylund.

'Keep your heads down,' he warned the two women and the preacher, before going over to the window himself. Out in the desert Nylund could see a row of riders heading their way, seven men in total, and a wagon being driven behind them. As Nylund watched they stopped, one rider breaking away to come toward the shack.

'Listen up you old fool.' Nylund grabbed Franklin Ford by the collar of his coat, pulling him up close. 'Now you don't say a word about us being here, understand?'

The man smiled at Nylund, his wide, inane grin resembling that of a drunkard.

'Won't he expect to come in?' asked the attorney.

'I don't think so, the old man doesn't live in here, but in the lean-to out back,' Nylund explained.

'So won't he find it strange that he comes out of the door?' the driver asked, nodding at Ford.

'That's a risk we have to take.'

The ambusher was coming closer, calling out.

'Ford, Ford, where are you, you old coyote?'

With one hand Nylund opened the door, and put the other flat on Ford's back, pushing him out through it.

'There you are, you old mule.'

From the corner of the window Nylund watched as the man climbed down from the horse. He didn't immediately recognize him from the ambush, but as he came closer Nylund remembered him as one of the men who had taken the gold from the roof of the stage.

Nylund's hand tightened on the stock of his rifle, it helped to defuse the anger he felt.

'We've got another job for you,' the man was enigmatic, 'and I believe you've something for us, ain't you?'

Franklin Ford stepped forward a pace and Nylund saw him nod his head. Things were going well, but for Nylund the worry wasn't yet over.

'Is it round the back, in the lean-to?'

Obviously the man wanted whatever valuables the Indians traded for the rifles.

Ford nodded again, he hadn't spoken yet, something which Nylund saw as a blessing. Taking a sharp intake of breath, Nylund watched as the man took Ford's arm to lead him to the rear of the building. Leaping across to the back wall of the shack, Nylund's feet banged on the bare wooden floor, making a clattering sound.

'What was that?'

Nylund heard the question clearly, but

Ford's answer came through the wall mumbled.

Desperately he hoped that the explanation was either incomprehensible or foolish, and that Ford had not given away the passengers' presence. Whatever he had said obviously satisfied the man, for nothing came of it.

Listening carefully, Nylund could only pick out the occasional word, none of which was spoken by Ford. The door of the lean-to was opened. After a few seconds it was shut again, with Ford and the desperado returning to the front of the shack. This time Nylund was extra careful as he crossed the floor, his movements silent; he didn't want to give himself away again.

'Yee haw!'

Ford's sudden shout unnerved Nylund, and he had to check himself from making an exclamation.

'Yee haw!'

It came again, this time not as unexpected. Shifting his position a little further to the left Nylund was closer to the window but the semi-darkness prevented him from being seen.

'We've got another wagon for you, Ford,' the man told him, ignoring the sudden yells he had let out. 'You can take that wagon to them?'

'Yep,' Ford nodded, slapping his hands together in excitement.

'And me and the boys will wait here until you come back.'

Nylund clenched the fist of his free hand, thumping it lightly against his forehead. This was the answer as to how Ford got the rifles to the Indians; the men brought them in the wagon and waited for it to be returned empty. Why Ford didn't hand over then what he had received in trade, Nylund couldn't figure; maybe the transaction was conducted on trust, that was the only explanation. It was impossible for the ambushers to stay here, for they would soon discover the passengers. Would Ford be able to dissuade them? If he could, would the men find it suspicious?

It felt like hours were passing as Ford paused before speaking.

'You can't stay here,' he laughed raucously. 'I already got people here.'

That was all Nylund needed. Swinging open the door and dropping the rifle, he reached out his arm and grabbing the back of Ford's collar, tugged him backwards and off-balance into the shack, at the same time drawing the Colt clear of its holster. Outside, the desperado swung round to face the doorway, his hand going down to grab his revolver. Nylund pulled the trigger of his own weapon before the man had even got a firm grip on his gun. With the lead piercing his chest, the bandit fell backwards onto the rough desert floor.

Clearing Ford from the doorway, Nylund slammed it shut. Grabbing a chair he tipped it up and jammed the door, putting the Colt back into its holster.

'Yee haw!' Franklin Ford brought up a knee and slapped it hard with an open palm. If nothing that had passed before had done so, this now proved the man to be totally crazy.

Yet Nylund found that he couldn't be angry. Ford had been put into an impossible position, one that even the sanest of men would have had difficulty with.

Ford moved to pull the chair away from the door, but Nylund grabbed at his arms to stop him.

'Let him go,' suggested the attorney, voicing a sensible idea in the circumstances.

Kicking out at one of the legs of the chair Nylund pulled it from the door. Ford seized the opportunity to escape, snatching the door open. The crazy man took just one step out before he was cut down in a hail of bullets, the force of which spun him around like a top. Despite his injuries he somehow managed a faint smile, then collapsed onto the ground, dead.

Quickly Nylund slammed the door shut again. Pushing the chair back into place, he drew a deep breath, and picking up the rifle, prepared himself for the inevitable fight.

TWELVE

Nylund risked taking a look out of the corner of the glassless window-frame, his effort immediately resulting in a hail of lead coming his way. Diving beneath the frame Nylund gave thought to the little he had managed to see. The wagon was still in place, but all the riders and horses were gone, with the team also having been taken from the wagon. It was from behind the wagon that Nylund guessed the shots were coming, with the men obviously using it for cover.

'You should have never let that poor man go,' the attorney's wife snapped at both Nylund and her husband.

'I agree,' announced the wife of the preacher.

'He wanted to go,' said the lawyer, 'it was his choice. You saw him yourselves, he went for the door.'

'Still, you should have stopped him,' his wife argued against logic.

'If he'd stayed here he would have done us harm,' Nylund stated. Still in position below the window, he put authority into his voice. 'And that's the last anyone is going to say about it. We don't need squabbles between ourselves.'

The stage driver came across the floor to Nylund, keeping himself low.

'What can you see?'

'Just the wagon, they're using that for cover, I think.'

'Which leaves us with a stalemate situation,' the driver said, telling Nylund what was obvious to him. 'While we're in here and they've got cover, neither side is going to achieve anything.'

'They're going to have to come out in the open eventually, and all we can do is wait.'

'Wait until nightfall?' the driver asked acidly. 'At which time they could be anywhere, behind us, beside us. We wouldn't know, they'd have the cover of darkness.'

'Let me try to talk to them; they'll see I'm not an advocator of violence,' the preacher suggested. 'Surely we can find a way where no more lives have to be lost.'

'Preacher, you wouldn't be able to get one word out before they shot you,' Nylund told him sharply. 'Their own man, Ford, couldn't even get that far.'

'Can't I try? For pity's sake, man,' his voice filling with emotion, the preacher continued to press his point, 'my one life against all of those here, it's not too much to give.'

'It's a life too many.' Nylund needed his concentration to be fixed on what was outside, and didn't want an enemy from within his own ranks to distract him from that task.

All was quiet outside and Nylund inched up the wall to take another look out through the window. The wagon was still there, too far away for Nylund to see clearly if men were hiding behind it. Suddenly, from its left, a man broke away, rifle at his side, running at an angle towards the side of the shack. Bringing the stock of his own weapon up to his shoulder, Nylund took aim, squeezing the trigger slowly. In the distance the man fell to the ground, to lie there immobile. So remote was the death from Nylund that he felt nothing at having killed another human being; it was no different to shooting bottles off a fence.

'Two down, six to go,' Nylund said coldly, ducking quickly as another hail of bullets came his way. 'At least now we're equal in number, if not firepower.'

Shots had slammed against the shack, but with its solid construction none of them penetrated the wall. The cabin's only vulnerable spot was the unglazed window-frame, but, as none of the occupants were in the direct line of fire, the occasional lead that whistled through slammed harmlessly into the rear wall. When that round of shots ceased, no more came. For an hour or more they sat or lay there, just waiting for the next crack of gunfire.

'Have they gone?' the attorney's wife asked.

'No, they won't be going anywhere,' Nylund answered. 'The difference between them and us being that they have a choice, we don't. They know that eventually we'll have to come out of here when our food and water is used up. Be it days, or weeks, they know we can't stay in here.'

'We might be here weeks?' The woman gasped, the thought appalling her.

'No, no.' Nylund almost had a chuckle in his voice, such was the stupidity of the question. 'They aren't going to hang around waiting for weeks, when, with the advantages they have over us, they could have us out of here, in some way or other, in hours.'

'In some way or other?' The attorney's wife repeated Nylund's words with a questioning inflection.

'Dead or alive, my dear.' The preacher answered her query, saving Nylund the trouble.

'Oh.' The woman spoke involuntarily, her

mind feverishly working on what she had been told.

As the time passed, one hour turning into two, then three, Nylund became increasingly bored, a boredom that made him tense. He was a man of action, not one who was comfortable in circumstances such as these. Were it not for the responsibility he held toward the other passengers, or had he been alone, Nylund would have been tempted to break out and flee across the desert, doing his best to avoid the inevitable onslaught of rifle fire.

If the ambushers were intelligent enough to try and defeat Nylund psychologically then they were having a slight success with their plan. Nylund thought it doubtful that this was what they were aiming for; the delay in them taking any other action was most likely because they were too dumb to think of a plan.

'Can't we bargain with them?' the preacher asked, his nerves, too, being worn down.

'The time for that has passed, if it ever

existed,' explained Nylund. 'With two of their men already dead, they're not going to look favourably on the offer of a pocket-watch and a few dollars.'

Slowly the day was beginning to pass, with Nylund counting the hours. Already they had been in the shack for eight hours. He wondered how much longer it would be until it was all over. Considering for a moment forcing the situation, he realized it would be a mistake, for neither he nor the stage driver had enough ammunition to keep up a very long volley of fire.

Dusk had begun to fall, and before long the semi-darkness that now existed in the shack would be totally black. With his thirst growing, Nylund edged across the floor to take a sip of water from the bucket that he had wisely brought inside.

'Have you any idea what's happening out there?' the stage driver asked Nylund as they sat alongside each other, the man lowering his voice to a whisper.

'No.' Nylund shook his head. 'But the

longer this goes on the more worried I become.'

They stayed where they were, leaning against the shack's rear wall, with Nylund stretching his legs, trying to restore some of the blood flow to them. Over the next hour darkness arrived completely, plunging the interior of the shack into blackness.

Nylund and the stage driver spoke in low voices, discussing the possibilities that faced them, both knowing that they could only respond to what was commenced against them, and not initiate it.

Suddenly, and without any warning, firing began. The shots concentrated on the window and whistled into the shack, causing everyone to duck. With the amount of lead being fired it was impossible for Nylund to get anywhere near the window and have a chance to return it. Instead he, like the rest of them, lay on the floor, waiting for the bombardment to stop. Whether it was a trick of his imagination or not, Nylund believed he could hear horses riding toward the shack; it couldn't be that the youngster had found help, for the firing was still aimed at the shack. When he had nearly dismissed it as an illusion, the sound grew louder, proving that it didn't exist only in his head.

The firing stopped, but the horses' hooves pounding the ground didn't. As Nylund began to move toward the window, he could see flaming torches outside, close by, their burning brightness lighting up the faces of the men who held them. Nylund drew his Colt, firing off a couple of loose rounds, neither hitting a target.

As Nylund neared the window the flaming torches came flying through the frame. Landing on the floor, they immediately set it alight. Snatching off his coat Nylund pounded at the tongues of flames licking at the tilted chair that was keeping the door shut. A flame shot up, evading the coat to catch hold of Nylund's left shirtsleeve. At this, the preacher was up from behind the turned-up table and beating out the flames on Nylund's arm with his bare hands. The pain of his burning arm was so bad that Nylund felt close to blacking out.

The fire was, meanwhile, growing fiercely. If left it threatened to burn out the shack. Grabbing their sole bucket of water, the driver threw it at the flames. His aim was perfect and they died instantly and he stamped on the few flickering embers to extinguish them.

'Thank you.' Nylund was truly grateful to the preacher. Though the burn was bad, it wasn't severe, due to the preacher's quick thinking and action. Wrapping his neckerchief around the blistering skin Nylund tied a tight knot, using his teeth to do so. There wasn't time at present to do anything fancy. Fortunately, it wasn't his gun arm, so Nylund could still shoot.

'There's not a lot of damage.' The stage driver surveyed the area where the fire had been, kicking through the ashes.

'I knew they had something in mind.' Nylund shook his head in despair at what could have been. 'We've got to block that window to prevent them from trying it again.'

The room was in darkness and Nylund was unable to look for anything with which to barricade the window, but memory suggested he would be unsuccessful anyway. The only item that would do was the table. It would be taking protection away from the women and the preacher, yet it would serve a better purpose at the window.

With the stage driver's help, Nylund lifted the table onto one end, carrying it across to the front wall where it blocked the window, leaving only a narrow gap running down either side, just enough room for the barrel of a rifle.

It wouldn't end there, they would be back, there was no doubt of that. Whether it would be that night, or the next day, Nylund didn't know. Despite the consequences, he hoped the attack would come soon, for tomorrow he would be tired, worn out by the recent events and a sleepless night.

Nylund didn't even allow his mind to

wander toward the prospect of the youngster reaching help and returning with it, there wasn't even the slightest chance of that happening.

The time had come, Nylund decided, for him to try and turn the tide of defeat that was heading their way. Darkness was a friend to both the ambushers and those in the shack, and it was a friend that Nylund was now going to call upon for help.

With the chair that had kept it shut now insecure after the fire, the door was open a gap, and with the wind increasing so would that gap widen; with no way to keep the door closed, Nylund realized that the chances they had were getting slimmer by the minute.

Reloading his Colt helped him acquire a determined state of mind, and with the revolver in his hand he felt a surge of energy running through him. No longer was he going to sit and let the fight come to him; he intended to take it to them. Finding the attorney in the darkness of the shack, Nylund pushed the rifle into his hands.

'Make good use of that if needs be.'

Without speaking further Nylund made his way to the door, opening it just wide enough to look out and listen for movement before stepping out into the night. Behind him there was a small thud as the door closed, with the driver scuffling about behind it.

The fresh air was pleasant to Nylund, and he took a few seconds out to take deep breaths. The interior of the shack had been stuffy, and the acrid smoke from the short-lived fire made it even more oppressive.

While he had no idea where the remaining six men were, Nylund had the advantage of them not knowing that he was on the prowl. Keeping his body close to the wall of the building, Nylund edged round to the rear. With his heart beating fast and his adrenalin flowing Nylund was preparing himself for whatever he might encounter.

There was the sound of heavy breathing, which made Nylund hold his own breath, suspecting that his own breathing was being echoed to his ears. The noise continued, and Nylund let out a silent sigh. He wasn't alone out here. Though trying to muffle any sound he made, the other man didn't need to be as cautious as Nylund. Bringing the Colt up close to the side of his face Nylund moved nearer to the source of the sound. Ahead of him, near to the well, Nylund could just about pick out a heavy shape. It stood stationary for a second, then walked toward Nylund. Fearing he had been spotted, Nylund stood perfectly still, not daring to move. He didn't want to give himself away.

So close was the desperado now that Nylund could smell the stale tobacco and whisky from his breath.

'One move, and I'll blow a hole in you,' Nylund whispered threateningly, digging the barrel of the Colt into the soft fat of the man's neck.

There was tension in the air, so heavy that it stank.

'Turn around,' Nylund ordered, allowing

the barrel to follow round to the back of the man's neck as he turned away from Nylund.

Reaching into the man's holster Nylund drew out a heavy Smith and Wesson; spinning it in his hand and catching hold of the barrel, he brought the butt down squarely on the man's head. A dull thud sounded, the man fell to his knees, and forward onto his face. Shoving the Smith and Wesson into his waistband, Nylund holstered his own Colt. Grabbing the unconscious man's coat he pulled him against the side wall of the shack; there was no need to tie him up, he wouldn't be coming round for several hours. The blow Nylund had delivered was hard enough to lay a buffalo low.

It was now five men to one. For Nylund the odds were getting much better, although when it came down to three to one he'd feel much more comfortable. If the ambushers had not been involved in a gun trade with the Indians, if they had not come to the shack, if they had not intended to stay while

Ford did his trading, if Nylund had been able to find help; then he still would have gone after the men. It was an awful lot of 'ifs', but the truth was that what Nylund was now doing, disposing of the men one by one was inevitable. Had he got the passengers to safety he would certainly have returned to the prairie to find the men, for when they ambushed the stagecoach they kindled a fire in him, one that could only be extinguished by the recovery of the stolen gold, and the capture, or deaths, of the thieves.

Grateful that the chance had come sooner rather than later, Nylund continued his search for the other men. To discover what the man he had just hit had been doing at the rear of the building was a priority. Nylund couldn't take the risk of there being another fire started. Once he had made his way silently towards where he believed the bandits to be, Nylund surveyed the area. It was dark, with not a flicker of flame to be seen, which relieved Nylund for he hoped that the danger for the others was over.

'Munroe, what are you doing?' a voice called, reaching Nylund as a low whisper.

For the second time Nylund had been mistaken for a man by the name of Munroe. Evidently it was the name of the man he had just felled. Having learnt his lesson before, Nylund wasn't going to claim he was the man.

'Munroe? Where are you?' This time the voice was louder and more urgent.

Nylund didn't know what to do. Did he reply in the hope of drawing the man closer, or stay quiet and pray that he came near enough for Nylund to strike?

'Munroe?' Coming closer, the man's tone showed he was becoming suspicious. If Nylund didn't do something soon to distract him, he was going to be put at a disadvantage.

Beneath Nylund's feet he could feel small stones, and he silently bent down, scooping several up in his palm. Bending his arm back he threw the stones toward the well, and was rewarded when they thudded against its wall.

'Munroe. There you are.'

The voice was now not so clear, as the man had his back to Nylund. Able to see the man, Nylund couldn't shoot. It would be too risky, for the sound of a gunshot would bring the whole darn lot of them down on him. As Nylund was raising the Smith and Wesson to bring it down on the back of the man's head the man turned. For a second his and Nylund's eyes locked, the man looking for familiarity in the face of the man near him. Realizing it wasn't Munroe he drew back a huge fist. Letting the revolver drop from his fingers Nylund pulled out his knife. As the man's fist came at him, Nylund slipped the punch and brought up the knife-blade, sticking it in between the man's ribs, and twisting the blade with a movement of the wrist.

Obligingly, the man fell forward onto the knife, and Nylund, stepping backwards, pushed him away. Using both hands, the pain of his left arm still bad, Nylund needed all of his strength to pull out the knife.

Nylund wasn't either proud or pleased that he had killed the man. He would have preferred just to have temporarily disabled him. But there hadn't been time. All the killings that had taken place made Nylund feel sick. He eased his conscience slightly by accepting that he was in a kill or be killed situation. None of them would have any compunction about pulling the trigger on Nylund.

Four men were still a threat to him and the stage passengers. It would only take one bullet to stop Nylund, so he couldn't afford to relax for even a second. Because he had had success until now, it didn't naturally follow it would continue.

Boom!

The sound of a single rifle shot shook Nylund down to his toes. It had been fired close by, but had not been aimed at him, coming from inside the shack. Forgetting all about his own well-being Nylund ran to the front of the shack, the safety of the passengers foremost in his mind. Drawing the

Colt, he came to the side of the door, finding it ajar. Reaching out his arm Nylund pushed on the door and it swung open with ease.

This time throwing caution to the wind, he leapt through the doorway. Facing him was the barrel of a rifle. Nylund holstered the Colt, breathing a sigh of relief when he saw that the stage driver was holding it.

'It's you, good. What happened?'

'He kicked the door open and ran in,' explained the stage driver, gesturing to the body on the floor. 'I guess he thought we'd be off our guard.'

'And he learnt otherwise.' Nylund slapped the driver on the shoulder. 'You did a good job.'

'Horses!' the preacher shouted by way of a warning.

'Everybody back from the door,' Nylund ordered, fearing another fire attack.

As the passengers scurried to the rear of the shack, Nylund went to the door. Firing loose rounds toward the sound of horses, knowing he would be lucky to score a hit in the darkness, he was only using it as a deterrent. Pulling back in, Nylund sheltered behind the wall as he reloaded the Colt. Listening before opening fire again, Nylund realized the horses were riding from, and not toward him.

'They're going!' the driver yelled in excitement. 'We chased them off.'

'It sure looks like it,' agreed Nylund, shaking his head in disbelief; incredibly, the other three had been frightened off.

Nylund figured that having their friends killed made them decide to flee rather than fight. They were escaping, but only for the time being, for if they took the gold with them, Nylund would soon be following.

'You know what this means, don't you?' the stage driver told the others excitedly. 'They've left us with the means to get to safety. They've taken three horses, but left us the others, and the wagon.'

'Let's be on our way,' suggested the attorney, eagerness in his voice.

'No,' Nylund stopped him. 'We'll be safer travelling by day. They've gone now, but that's not to say they won't set up another ambush.'

'You're right,' the lawyer agreed. The logic of Nylund's suggestion was easy to see.

'I'm just about out on my feet,' Nylund drawled. Tiredness had caught up with him.

Finding a reasonably comfortable corner, he settled down to sleep, asking the driver to wake him at dawn.

A bright and early morning sun woke Nylund; he rubbed his eyes. The table had been removed from the window and returned to an upright position in the centre of the shack, allowing the light in.

'We were going to dig graves.' The driver spoke quietly to Nylund. 'But we thought we'd wait until you were with it.'

Nylund nodded and stood. It was the Christian thing to do; they couldn't just ride away without burying the men.

Without a word passing between them the

four men went out of the shack. At the rear of the building they found a shady spot suitable for the burial, and while the driver began to dig, Nylund went back to the front of the shack to collect the body of Franklin Ford.

'You thought we'd gone,' a man's voice spoke to Nylund, causing him to look up sharply. 'The other two went, but I wasn't going to run.'

There was no doubting who the man was. Nylund recognized him as the one who had kept guard over them while the coach was being robbed. The man had been unstable then. He would, if anything, be even more disturbed now.

Nylund saw the man's hand go to his holster, and Nylund reached for his own Colt.

For the first time in his life Nylund had met someone faster. With his own revolver still not clear of the holster, the man standing opposite had his fully drawn. Nylund prepared himself for what was about to happen. It was ironic that they had got so close to a safe getaway, and then have this happen.

His heart pounding, Nylund remained outwardly calm, though he took a sharp breath at the crack of a shot. With blood spreading across the front of his shirt the man standing across from him slumped to his knees, the revolver in his hand going off and blowing a hole in the ground.

Nylund swung round on his heel to see who had fired the shot that had undoubtedly saved his life.

'I think that's made us even, don't you?' The attorney smiled as he handed Nylund the freshly-fired rifle.

Nylund shook the attorney gratefully by the hand.

'I guess I had you wrong.'

'No.' The attorney smiled sheepishly. 'I was wrong, and you put me right.'

With his wife clinging lovingly to his arm, the man walked away. Taking a deep breath, a surprised Nylund heard it come out as a sigh. Then he shook himself into action; there was much to be done.

The publishers hope that this book has given you enjoyable reading. Large Print Books are especially designed to be as easy to see and hold as possible. If you wish a complete list of our books please ask at your local library or write directly to:

Dales Large Print Books
Magna House, Long Preston,
Skipton, North Yorkshire.
BD23 4ND